THE COLOR OF NOON

The Color of Noon

And Other Stories

Eugene Datta

The Color of Noon, and other stories
Copyright © 2024 Eugene Datta
First Edition

Paperback ISBN: 978-1-947175-62-4

Library of Congress Control Number:
2024947548

Cover art by Eugene Datta
Author photo by Anastasia Datta
Cover formatted by Jacob Arms

Published by Serving House Books
Lawrence Landing Company
Raleigh, North Carolina 27609
United States of America
www.servinghousebooks.com

Serving House Books is a proud member of

Independent Book Publishers Association
 and
Community of Literary Magazines and Presses

SERVING HOUSE BOOKS

In memory of Abhijit Gupta,

who left early

CONTENTS

Acknowledgments

New Life   1

Epitaph   28

Rain   37

I Can Be His Proxy   48

The Color of Noon   64

Movie Star   81

Rules of Waking Life   97

Hammer and Sickle   105

Fifteen Days   119

A Minute's Silence   141

About the Author

ACKNOWLEDGMENTS

My gratitude to the editors of the magazines in which some of these stories, sometimes in earlier versions, first appeared: *The Bombay Literary Magazine*, "Hammer & Sickle"; *Common Ground Review*, "I Can Be His Proxy"; *The Bangalore Review*, "Epitaph". I am particularly thankful to Janet Bowdan (of *CGR*) and Sucharita Dutta-Asane (of *TBR*) for the care they took with my stories, catching what I missed. A very early version of the title story had appeared as "Win" in *dimsum, a journal of good reading,* while an early version of "Movie Star" appeared as "Maharaja" in *Persimmon: Asian Literature, Arts and Culture.*

I am indebted to Stiftung Laurenz-Haus for their generous support, which made possible at least some of the work that appears here. I am grateful, also, to all those who read drafts of many of these stories and generously shared their opinions and insights, particularly Kunal Basu, Steven Helmling, George Bilgere, and Mita Kapur.

Immense gratitude to Kunal Basu for being an unfailing source of inspiration, encouragement and support. And thanks to everyone at Serving House Books, especially Bill Lawrence for the faith he showed in my writing by plucking my manuscript out of his slush pile and shaping it into this book.

Finally, as always, I'm grateful to my family—Natalia, Anastasia and Yannick. It is thanks to them that I get to write.

NEW LIFE

Mihir Jacob waited tables at Café Deluxe on Sudder Street six days a week, went to church Sunday mornings and sang with Five Mad Monkeys for fun when they rehearsed Sunday evenings, and wanted to continue doing that for the rest of his life. Until the day Ravi Roy told him he looked like Michael Jackson.

"If MJ had straight hair, he'd look absolutely like you," he said. "You have the same face and the same body. And you can sing, too. And look at your name—what a coincidence, man!"

If anyone else had said that, Mihir would have just let it out the left ear and forgotten about it the next second. But Ravi Roy was no ordinary man. He played the drums for the Monkeys, and was their band leader. Not just that, his father used to know Cliff Richard when he was still Harry Webb. They were friends. And Ravi's mother, a Khasi lady from Shillong, was a piano teacher at Loreto. Plus, he was the only one Mihir knew who had copies of Rolling Stone arriving at his doorstep straight from America. So, if anyone knew anything about music and musicians, it was him.

MJ, Mihir thought. *Of course!*

And Ravi was right about the other things, too—the eyes, the mouth, the color of the skin, the skinniness.

Standing in front of the *BAD* album cover poster in Raghunath Mishra's shop later that day, and stealing glances at his reflection on the showcase, Mihir nodded to himself. He wondered why it never occurred to him or anybody else before, but now that it was as clear as daylight, he couldn't go on being the same man anymore—the half Bengali, half Anglo-Indian Sudder Street waiter who could sing a song or two and was light on his feet, but didn't have the balls to get on stage and do it like the Monkeys.

Things had to change.

First the hair, Mihir decided, since that was the only obvious difference between him and Michael Jackson. And it made much more sense for him to get his hair curled than to expect the big man to straighten his. So he went to Tip Top Beauty Parlor (Ladies & Gents) to talk to Selim Ali, whom he'd once heard say to another customer that he knew how to curl hair. If he couldn't do it, Mihir would go somewhere else—there were a thousand and one saloons and parlors within a square kilometer of his neighborhood, and someone somewhere would know how to do it. If not, he'd ask his friend, philosopher and guru to ask one of his uncles in America to send a hair curling kit. He remembered how Ravi had done it once.

"Did you ever do it before?" Mihir asked Selim, not sure a guy who still wore bellbottoms, and hair like Hindi film heroes from the Seventies, could do such a hip thing like curling hair.

"Of course!" Selim said. "Ask the Parsi auntie from your next-door house."

"Mrs. Mistry?" Mihir frowned. "But her hair is straighter than mine!"

"Her fault," Selim shrugged. "She hated the smell."

The story was that Mrs. Mistry had run out of the shop in broad daylight with curlers hanging from one side of her head, and never came back. A friend of Selim's wife had later found out that she went to a parlor on Free School Street to get rid of the curls he'd put into her hair.

"Not many curls, you understand? But they were so strong she had to go to an *expert* to get rid of them!" Selim bragged. "Ask her, and if she's honest she'll tell you." He said it was fine if Mihir just paid for the kit and "extra something"—he'd do it for a friend.

Mihir never thought of Selim as a friend, but if he could fix his hair and didn't make him pay through the nose, why not?

That was how Mihir Jacob's journey to his new life started in Tip Top Beauty Parlor (Ladies & Gents).

It happened on a Thursday. The café was closed because the owner's grandfather had died and everyone on staff (except him) had gone to the crematorium. But like all things in his old life, the start to his new one wasn't easy. Barbers and butchers don't work on Thursdays. Selim said he'd open the shop for him in the afternoon. "After one," he said. "Come in through the back door. I'll be inside. It will take an hour."

It took almost three. Selim kept fumbling and dropping the curlers, and cursing under his breath. It was obvious he was not the expert he'd pretended to be, but it was too late to do anything about that. So Mihir just sat there clenching his jaw, angry at himself for buying into Selim's bullshit and not going to a better place. It was also unbearably hot and stuffy in there. The front door was closed, and the back door was too narrow and small to make any difference. And the ceiling fan just wobbled and squeaked, hardly moving the air. Sitting there like that, his body and face covered in sweat, and staring at the disaster unfolding on his head, and inhaling the pissy smell descending from there, he wondered how in God's good name he could ever get back to looking like himself again. *Forget Michael Jackson!* He thought about Mrs. Mistry and how she'd escaped, and felt a sudden urge to spring from the chair, tear himself free from the ugly, sticky clutch of Selim's hands and do exactly what she'd done. The urge was so strong it hit him like a bolt of lightning, its veins of energy shot through the veins in his body. Mihir gripped the armrests to stay still.

When Selim finally finished, he felt like throttling the man. What stared at him from the mirror was a furry dog's behind with a man's face that vaguely looked like his. The only way anyone could make it look like *his* head again was by shaving off that tangled mess. Mihir was beside himself with anger. But instead of lifting the chair and slamming it against the mirror, which he didn't have the strength to do anyway, or punching Selim in the face (*which* he easily could), he just shifted his gaze to the man's face in the mirror and said, "What the hell is this?"

Selim looked like he couldn't believe his ears, his proud smile vanished from his face.

"Hunh?" Mihir asked again. "What did you do?"

Selim stared at his hair in the mirror like he was looking for an answer there. He was standing right next to him, but was looking at him in the mirror. Mihir never got this thing about barbers—they always talk to you in the mirror, even when you're closer than that sheet of glass! Funny. But anyway, for now Selim wasn't talking. He just kept looking at Mihir's hair, looking beaten and scared, like someone waiting to be punished for a crime they knew they'd committed.

Finally, he said, "I'm sorry you don't like it. You don't have to pay."

That did something to Mihir. All his anger vanished in a blink, like shy crabs on a beach, and he felt sorry for the man. He felt sorry for making him feel so bad and guilty that he didn't want any money from him. *All that work plus the stuff he had to buy!* Mihir of course would *never* not pay someone for their work. He'd learned that from his father, CC Jacob (CC for Christopher Clarence). Even when he hated what his tailor had done, or had to clean up after the sweeper, he always paid them their due. He'd let them know he wasn't happy, but gave them their money even when he couldn't use the fruit of their labor. "You may not *like* what they did," he told Mihir once, "but don't forget it cost them time and sweat. And you're not a man if you don't pay for that!"

Speaking of *man*, CC Jacob was one like no other Mihir had ever known. It's *his* rotten luck that he had to die so early. If he hadn't, Mihir would have had a different life. His father wanted him to join the merchant navy, and if he was around a few more years Mihir would now be sailing from one foreign port to another—Singapore, Tokyo, New York—making money like his cousin, Joe Mayo, instead of serving coffee and toast and omelet and banana shake to unwashed backpackers in Café Deluxe. Joe's father had died early, and CC Jacob, being the man that he was, had taken him, his older sister's son, under his wing and paid for his education, and then sent him to the merchant navy. He wanted to do the same for his own son but died before Mihir could even finish school. *Fate!* What could anyone do about that? So Mihir had decided early on that the only way he could make up for his father's absence in his adult life was by following his advice. CC Jacob would be proud if he knew just how faithfully his son did that.

Mihir took out a five-rupee note and two tenners, which equaled the amount Selim would have charged if he wasn't a "friend", put the money on the counter, and without another word walked out of the shop.

It was almost four, but it was so hot there weren't too many people outside. And most pedestrians had their heads hidden under big umbrellas, which, Mihir *hoped*, limited their view of other pedestrians. Looking how he was now, he didn't want to be seen by anyone, especially anyone he knew. He walked as fast as he could, aware of his hair, *feeling* it like never before. It wobbled like ribbon weed in a stream, or a mass of wire coils, each strand tugging at the skin of his scalp. He felt like he was carrying an unsteady load on his head. Hurrying past a rickshaw parked outside the tiny egg roll shop with its shutter halfway down, he recognized the rickshaw-wallah. It was Baburam. Luckily, he was asleep. Before turning into the narrow alley on the right, he couldn't help throwing a quick glance at Raghunath Mishra's shop on the other side of the road. The man was standing outside, smoking. Mihir was sure Raghunath hadn't seen him. Even if he had, he certainly couldn't tell it was Mihir. The only person who might have recognized him was the madman who roamed the neighborhood all day. Mihir had almost bumped into him as he came out of the alley and turned left. The man was standing at the corner with his back to the courier office, babbling to himself. He burst into a wild laugh as their eyes met—a few black teeth in a gaping mouth, and the sound of a hyena. "Shut up!" Mihir hissed at him.

An auto-rickshaw came hurtling toward them, blaring its horn as it sped past. The madman laughed again. Mihir felt his heart racing.

Back home a few minutes later, he avoided looking at himself in the mirror. He took off his shoes and unbuttoned his shirt, then picked up a towel to wipe the sweat off his face, body and arms. He drank a glass of water and sat down at the table, slightly out of breath. Moma (his aunt, Modesty Mayo, Joe's mother) wasn't at home. He wondered what she'd say if she saw him now. *And Joe?* He'd have made his life miserable. Mihir wouldn't even have thought about doing such a thing if he was in town. He was sure about that! He tried to imagine his father's reaction. *What would he say?* The door to Mrs. Das's flat, which was opposite theirs, opened, and then closed. Mihir was glad the woman hadn't rung the bell, which she frequently did. She and Moma were friends. He poured himself another glass of water. He couldn't imagine his father being an older man, which he would be if he was still around. *What happened to your hair, Mihir?* he imagined him saying, laughing his big hearty laugh. He imagined his father leaning over to ruffle his hair, which he'd been fond of doing, his fingers now getting caught in the curls.

When Mihir finally stood in front of the mirror, his glance shifting from his own reflection to the Michael Jackson poster and back, he couldn't believe his eyes. Now he felt even sorrier that he'd screamed at Selim. It was as if, looking for the devil's den, he'd just wandered into God's backyard! The curls that had made him look like a muddy mongrel in Selim's shop, suddenly looked so good they made Mihir Jacob look like a perfect copy of the pasha named Michael Jackson—the *real* MJ.

"Selim, you're the best!" Mihir said loudly, smiling. "And you, too, Ravi Roy!" He turned this way and that, tilted his head up and down, looking at himself from as many different angels as he could.

That night he couldn't sleep. Because of the hair. Because his new life depended on it, and he couldn't afford to mess it up by putting his head on the pillow. And he couldn't stop thinking about what he *knew* was waiting to happen. The minute he'd walk out of the house in the morning, *boom!* Even the dogs outside their gate would look at him differently. Now, at the Monkeys' rehearsals, it wouldn't be just "Mihir, let's have that MJ move one more time," or "Let's do 'I'm bad'!" It was going to be "MJ! MJ! MJ!"—they'd go completely crazy. And Ravi—oh, Ravi would be so proud he'd probably ask him to join the band. He'd probably change their name to Six Mad Monkeys. Or even better, *MJ & Five Mad Monkeys!* And in the streets whoever looked in his direction wouldn't know what had hit them. They wouldn't know whether to believe their own eyes or not. And when he'd get into those pants and that jacket, and those shoes, and get on stage....

The dream felt so real Mihir couldn't close his eyes even for a minute that night.

Pappu was the first one to notice. He was dusting one of the corner tables, and turned to look when he heard Mihir walk in.

The boy froze, his jaw dropped open, eyes popping out of his head. Mihir lifted his sunglasses to wink at him, then walked into the changing room-cum-store.

Shivshankar was getting into his grubby chef's outfit and Dinesh, already in his dung-green Café Deluxe uniform, was organizing one of the shelves. Mihir switched on a light, pretending he hadn't seen either man. He couldn't wait for them to see his hair, his new look. The dogs hadn't bothered to turn their heads when he walked past them, which put a damper on his mood first thing in the morning. Okay, they were *dogs*, but no human being had bothered to look either. But then, it was so early he hadn't crossed paths with too many people other than a few rickshaw-wallahs and milkmen—what would *they* know? So apart from Pappu's reaction, he hadn't seen any results yet.

He walked to his corner of the room without looking in any direction, opened his locker and started to fuss with the things inside. Shivshankar was still putting on his clothes. *A one-eyed goat could finish the Bible in half that time!* And Dinesh was still going about his own business. Not a peep from either of them. *Such blind people!* Mihir thought.

"What happened to your hair?" Shiv yawned as Mihir walked past him to get into the loo.

"Michael Jackson!" Pappu squealed from the door.

Shiv had to just turn his head in the boy's direction for him to vanish instantly behind the swing door. Then, slowly rolling up the sleeves of his sweaty chef coat and shaking his head, he said, "I hope *you* don't think so?"

The man couldn't be more than six or seven years older than Mihir, but he acted as if he'd gone to school with Indira Gandhi and his farts made more sense than other people's words. But if he was really so smart, Mihir wondered why he wasn't in a better place in life than the Café Deluxe kitchen! He liked his job less than Mihir did his and complained all the time, which *Mihir* never did, so why didn't he go look for a job at the Writers' where he claimed he knew everyone? Mihir had come close to asking him that more than once, just to put him in his place, and make him stop trashing people around him, but held back for fear of hurting his feelings. *Who knew what his story was!*

"Or do you?" Shiv was looking at him as if he had glasses on, and was looking over them for a better view. The smirk on his face was the exact one he always had on when he talked someone down.

All the anticipation and excitement that had built up in Mihir started to seep out of him—*psss*, like that. Like a slow tire leak. But he wasn't going to show it and get laughed at. So, as hard as it was, he pretended he didn't understand Shiv, and with a straight face and a chapati-flat voice said, "What do you mean?"

Even before the words came out of his mouth, he knew how lame they were going to sound. But he blurted them anyway, hoping they'd buy him the time he needed to prepare for a better reply.

"You *know* what I mean."

Mihir never thought much of himself. He knew he wasn't too bright; he'd failed English, math, and chemistry in CBSE and never set foot in a college. He wasn't anywhere near his father when it came to smarts, or his friend Ravi, who was sharp as a brand-new kitchen knife, but no one he knew made him feel as stupid and small and worthless as this bugger did.

"You mean this?" Mihir said with a wobbly voice, pointing a finger at his head.

Before Shiv could open his mouth again, they heard the firecracker voice of their boss, Chandan Das (CD, as Mihir secretly called him; *CD, the man who owned CD, the shop*). He asked Pappu where everybody was, and within a second burst in through the swing door, not giving either of them the chance to move.

"What's going on?" he barked, turning his head from one side to another and back, fast, like a crow that had landed somewhere strange. "Why is it so dark in here? What are the lights for?" He reached for the switchboard and slapped the rest of the lights on. "What are you guys doing? Where's Raju?"

Raju was CD's cousin. He handled the cash desk until around eleven thirty, when CD returned from his "other work," whatever that was. He was about Mihir's age, quiet and hardworking, and *nice*. He didn't throw his weight around even though he was related to the boss.

"Must be on the way," Shiv said, sounding like his voice was suddenly clogged up with melted sugar. He was always like that when he talked to the boss, all his cockiness carefully hidden, saved for the rest of the staff.

"Why haven't you changed yet?" he asked Mihir. "Any idea what time it is?"

Mihir never liked facing the man when he arrived in the morning. He was always in a bad mood, every single day. Mihir wondered if it was his wife—if he had fights with her every morning. Or with anyone else in his big family—parents (*even grandfather*, until a couple of days ago), brother, sister-in-law, nephew, niece. Once he'd asked Raju if that was the case. And Raju being *Raju*, just smiled and shrugged, and said he didn't know. *Who knew what the story was!* But as nice and kind as CD was as a boss, he was a monster when he arrived. For the first half-hour or so, Mihir tried to stay out of his way. But today he was glad the man had barged in on them, shutting up *Shit*shankar. Being screamed at by the boss was nothing compared to what this man was putting him through.

Mihir pointed to the toilet sheepishly, as if asking for the boss's permission to use it. Just then the door swung open and Raju walked in, distracting CD and giving Mihir the chance to disappear. He slipped into the toilet in rat speed and quickly closed the door behind him, glad that CD hadn't noticed his hair. If there was anyone he did *not* want to notice the change, it was him. *Oh, so you were busy curling your hair when I was burning my grandfather, right?* Mihir imagined him saying.

The stink in the toilet was so bad, so much worse than Selim's hair curling goo, it kept making his morning tea and biscuits climb back up the food pipe. Luckily, he didn't have to stay too long. He couldn't hear CD's voice anymore, and the only noise in the kitchen was of Shiv and Dinesh getting ready for the day, so he knew the coast was clear. Boss had left after instructing them to pack breakfast for twenty-two people, which Bhagwan, his man Friday, would pick up in an hour. Every time he had guests at home, he made Shiv and Dinesh cater for them.

The store was well-stocked. Nothing had been used the day before because the café was closed, so they could start right away. Raju made a trip to Aggarwal & Sons Grocery in New Market to replenish the stock of bread and butter, as Dinesh and Shiv got the parcels ready. Mihir was surprised he wasn't asked to do anything; CD hadn't left any instructions for him. In his old life (*which ended for good yesterday*), he wouldn't have worried about that—whom CD asked to do what depended on his morning mood, and it didn't have any effect on things later in the day. But today Mihir wasn't so sure. *Maybe the hair pissed him off, who knows!* he thought.

It was almost eight thirty when the first customer showed up. It was David, a man from New Zealand, six-foot-six or so and matchstick-thin. He bent his head down to walk through the door, like he was getting into a tiny hut or something. Mihir had a little chat with him a few days ago, and found out that it was his first trip to Calcutta. He was staying at Maria. "Why not Fairlawn?" Mihir had asked. "Cheaper," he said. *Sure!* Sudder Street had two types of tourists—the Fairlawn type and the non-Fairlawn type, which was most of them. Anyway, so David was the first one to walk in.

"Good morning," Mihir said.

"Morning." David smiled and sat down. "Chai, please," he said.

"And toast with butter and jam?"

"Yes, please," David nodded with a smile. He opened his faded backpack to take out his things, which usually were a couple of maps (he read maps like schoolchildren read books while getting ready for exams), a tenth-hand Lonely Planet on India, and a notebook.

By the time Mihir was back with the toast and the tea, David had started scribbling on his notebook. He lifted his head to say thanks and quickly went back to writing, no sign of him having noticed Mihir's hair. *A giraffe with bad eyes*, Mihir thought to himself. *Why else would he bend down like that on his notebook?*

Bill and Annette came next. Both were old-timers. They'd been coming to Café Deluxe for as long as Mihir had been working there. Bill was from England, although he said his father was an Anglo-Indian from Calcutta. And Annette was from someplace in Europe, but lived in South Africa and sounded as if she too was English. For the last few weeks, the two of them and Lambu (everyone at the café called David *Lambu* because of his height) had been the first ones to show up every morning.

"Moorning!" Bill said. Funny guy, always said moo instead of hello—not to everyone, but to people he knew in Sudder Street, which were many, including almost all the rickshaw-wallahs. He'd pucker his mouth like when people blow rings of cigarette smoke, doing it with the same care. And whoever knew Bill, did the same when they saw him. That was the extent of his communication with many in Sudder Street. If someone *he* didn't know did it to him, which happened now and then because he was famous for his moos, he was thrilled to bits.

"Moorning," Mihir replied with a nod, trying to pull out a chair so that Annette could get to the one next to the window, where she liked to sit when she came for breakfast. Bill had already sat down. He was looking at Mihir, mouth pursed, nodding his head. "So, omelet, toast and tea for you?" Mihir asked, feeling trapped in Bill's stare, so self-conscious that he could barely hear his own words.

"Good one!" Bill said, still nodding. "Cost a lot of money, I'm sure?"

"What?"

"The wig!" Bill gestured with his head.

"It's not a wig, Bill!" Annette chimed in, looking at Mihir's head. "What's wrong with you? He just got his hair curled."

"Is that right?" The man looked as if it was his life's biggest surprise. No telling if he was really surprised or was faking it to make fun of Mihir, who felt like an idiot anyway, as if he'd been caught with his fly open.

He turned around to see if anyone was close enough to hear any of this. CD wasn't there yet, but Mihir was worried about Shiv overhearing, or Raju. Luckily, no one was within earshot. Except Lambu, who was busy with his maps, and Lonely Planet, and notebook—he didn't care about anything else anyway.

"The same for you?" Mihir asked Annette, deciding not to meet Bill's eyes or answer him, or even ask him again if omelet, toast and tea, which he ordered every day, was what he wanted. He wanted to leave their table before either of them had a chance to say another word about his hair, even if it was going to be complimentary. Even if it was what he'd been dying to hear since he got out of the house in the morning.

"Yes, please." Annette smiled.

"For me too, please," Bill said, and then, as Mihir turned to leave, "Moo!"

He liked the guy, and mooed back at him all the time, even though sometimes it made him feel like a retarded cow. He did it because Bill liked it. He also laughed at all his jokes, whether he understood them or not (and he didn't understand a lot of them because of that funny accent of his). What he didn't like was the man's reaction to his hair. *A Wig? What kind of rat shit was that? A goat with its eyes and brains in the right places could tell it wasn't a wig!* He just wanted to embarrass Mihir, make him look like an idiot, a little Indian idiot with fake hair. *Not fair!* Mihir shook his head as he walked to the kitchen.

At nine, the kitchen looked, smelled and sounded like it normally did much later in the day. Smoke from the partly-burned slices of bread for the boss's twenty-two guests hung like fog around the tube lights. The grease-padded exhaust fan sounded as if it was drowned in a muddy drain. Raju and Bhagwan were putting the breakfast parcels and tea flasks in two jute shopping bags. Shiv was watching them, taking sips from a cup of tea and wiping his sweaty face with a dish towel (which he also used for the dishes, and God knew what else). Dinesh was putting away the things Raju had brought from the grocery store, grunting every time he had to bend to pick up something. And Pappu was sitting on the floor next to the fridge, chopping onions and rubbing his teary eyes.

"Omelet, toast and tea—two!" Mihir said without looking at anyone, but loudly enough for everyone in the kitchen to hear him.

Shiv didn't stir; he kept watching Raju and Bhagwan fuss with the parcels. "Oey, onion!" he barked at Pappu moments later, then said to Raju, "Leave it to him and go to the counter. His name's Bhagwan—he'll figure it out!"

"It's done," Raju said gently, and then to Bhagwan, gesturing, "Hold the bags like that, okay? Make sure the stuff doesn't tilt over. Come!" He held the swing door open for the man.

As Mihir followed Raju out of the kitchen, he noticed Shiv lift his head and throw a scowling glance at him. But he didn't say anything. He didn't make any other comment the rest of that day, which, like most Fridays, had been a busy one. Some of the regulars seemed to notice Mihir's hair, but no one said anything. Except Ahava, this pretty, young Israeli woman with curly brown hair that was so long it reminded Mihir of village women. She was always in a sleeveless t-shirt and wrinkled pajamas, with black glass bangles on her wrists and rubber flipflops, also black. No matter what time of day or night Mihir saw her, she looked like she'd just got out of bed.

"Wow," she smiled. "I like your new hair!"

Mihir couldn't believe his ears. "Thanks," he said, hoping no one else had heard her.

The café was full and quite noisy, and Ahava had a soft voice. Sometimes, he had to lean closer to hear what she was saying. *But not today.* He'd heard her loud and clear. He smiled, looking at her—her guava-green eyes and beautiful, sweet mouth. In his head, *sweet* was a word linked forever to the banana pancakes Moma made at home, the stuff he'd grown up eating, or the tea Dinesh made for the staff at the café, or how Tiwari's laddus tasted. Mihir could never imagine using the word sweet to describe how anyone *looked*, especially how their mouth looked, but that was the *only* word that came to his mind every time he saw Ahava. *Sweet, sweet, sweet—* that was how she and her smiling mouth looked. Mihir felt like a fly trapped in a gob of molasses. Once Boss had caught him while he was in such a state. He'd taken Mihir aside and said, "If you want to stare at white women, go see a film in Society, don't do it here!" Mihir had never gone to Society, but had seen enough vulgar posters with that cinema hall's name on them to know what kind of movies they showed. He was so embarrassed he couldn't look either Boss or Ahava in the eye for a few days.

Luckily, the man wasn't there when Ahava came today, but Mihir was worried just the same. Ever since Boss's mention of Society, his fly-in-molasses condition around this woman had worsened. Now, he noticed more than just her hair, and mouth, and smile. Now he saw that she never wore a bra, and that, depending on where and how she sat, and how she moved her arms, eating or drinking or reading something, or talking to someone, and where *he* was in the room, he could see more of her body than her shirts were meant to show.

"What would you like to have today?" Mihir asked.

From the way her smile changed as she reached for the menu, he could tell that Ahava wouldn't have minded a small chat. *But who knew which way that might go!* Plus, Boss could show up at any moment. If he found Mihir chumming up with her, new hair and all, *and not having gone to the crematorium for his grandfather's funeral*, and especially after what had happened in the morning, the first day of his new life could very well be his last day at work. So, although he didn't *want* to interrupt that smile, which was meant *just* for him, and wished he could look at those eyes looking at him a bit longer, he was relieved that he'd managed to shift her focus to the menu.

"Okay, let's see," Ahava said. As she read the menu, she ran her fingers through the ends of her hair, and then coiled a bunch of it around her right forefinger, her head slightly tilted to the left. She had this habit of combing, twirling, and braiding the ends of her hair while she read, and Mihir loved to watch her do that. Waiting for her to place the order, Mihir couldn't help looking down at the neckline of her top, the way her breasts rose against its thin cotton, and no bra or anything to hold them back. If Ahava had taken a minute longer to decide what she wanted, Mihir would have fainted. He would've just collapsed on the floor near her feet—*dhurrum*, like that, with his tray, order-pad and pencil. He was seeing stars when she looked up and said, with that smile, "Okay, a banana shake and a vegetable sandwich...please. Thanks!"

He'd moved hardly a foot or two from her table when Boss walked in. Mihir's heart missed a beat, but CD looked like he hadn't seen him.

Thank God!

It was such a close shave, Mihir was left in a fearful daze the rest of that day. Suddenly, things didn't seem as stable and predictable anymore. Anything could happen at any moment. If this really was his new life, it hadn't started the way he'd dreamed about it.

"You're not going to church with me looking like that," Moma said.

Mihir had just come home, washed up and sat down to eat dinner. She'd gone to visit her husband's sister, Dorothy Thapa, Thursday afternoon and stayed there overnight. As long as Dorothy's husband, an army major from Darjeeling, was alive, Moma hardly ever visited her sister-in-law. She was never too fond of Major Thapa, who, being a Nepali and an army guy, wasn't much of a Christian in her book. But now she went to her place several times a month, and stayed over every now and then. She'd never admit it, but she always mixed with people, or *didn't*, based on whether they were Christian or not. And for people like Major Thapa, even being Christian wasn't enough. Like his own mother. Mihir remembered what Joe had told him when he was hardly eleven or twelve: "My mum didn't want your dad to marry your mum because she was a Hindu."

He was six years older than Mihir, but behaved like his jealous twin and put him down whenever he could. And that was the most hurtful thing Joe had ever said to him. Mihir had been so shocked he couldn't say a word. Not because Joe said his mother was Hindu, which he knew she wasn't. And even if she was, who cared, she was his *mother. But he said Moma didn't want Dad to marry her!* It was *that* that'd shocked and surprised and hurt Mihir the most. Because that meant she was unwanted in the family, and as *her* son, so was he. He remembered that for the first time, he couldn't go to Moma and complain, hoping for support and reassurance, as he'd always done before. Although his father was still around, Mihir didn't say anything to him. For fear that he'd ask who had told him that, and he'd have to tell the truth, and then who knew what would've happened! So he just sat on it. And after his father died, he'd thought once or twice about asking Moma if what Joe had told him was true. But he never did that. One reason was, he'd never heard her mention his mother. She'd never let the word Lila (his mother's name) come out of her mouth, at least not in front of Mihir. And the few times he'd heard someone else mention his mother to her, she looked as if she wasn't sure who they were talking about.

So he *knew* that she wasn't too fond of his mother. Also, by then Mihir had found out that his mother was really baptized *after* she met his father. It had cropped up by chance one day as his father was talking about Father Claudius, who'd just died. This was a year and a half before his own death. He was talking about how long he'd known Father Claudius, and what a blessing he'd been to the family. "He was the one who'd helped with your mother's RCIA," he said. "Then he officiated our marriage, baptized Joe, presided at Mike Mayo's funeral, baptized you—did a lot for us, that man!" Mike Mayo was Joe's father, who'd died when Mihir was only two. But he had no idea what RCIA was, and why his mother needed that. "Rite of Christian initiation of adults," his father told him. "You do that when somebody becomes a new member of the church. Your mother wasn't a Catholic, and she wanted to be one."

Then Joe was right! Mihir thought.

The dining table stood in the passage-cum-verandah-cum-kitchen, at one end of which was the main door, and the bathroom at the other. The two bedrooms were side by side, like classrooms in a school. The one near the door was Mihir's, and the other, close to the bathroom, was Moma's. And between the two doors was the table. The tube light above the picture of Jesus (who watched over all their meals, trips to the bathroom, their comings and goings, and Moma's daily half-opened-door-to-half-opened-door gossip with Mrs. Das) was less than a week old, and shone with such brightness it made the whole place look shabbier and sadder than it normally did. It also showed Moma what she otherwise might not have noticed until the next morning. Now she sat opposite him with a face wrinkled in disgust.

"Did you hear me?"

Mihir tore a large piece of cold, leathery naan and dipped it into the greasy mutton curry. From the look and smell of the food, he could tell Moma had picked it up from Sher Khan, the small takeaway place at the end of their street. Chewing noisily, he nodded at her.

"Did you see your face in the mirror?"

Mihir nodded again, his mouth bulging.

"What does it look like?" Moma's face twisted with irritation.

He swallowed the food, wiped his mouth with a tissue, and said, "Michael Jackson."

Moma looked like she couldn't believe her ears.

Unlike many women her age, especially her "church sisters", for most of whom music began and ended with the choir of St. Mary's, she knew the names of not just Dean Martin, Frank Sinatra and Cliff Richard (who was the God of Music if you were Anglo Indian), but also of

Madonna, Lionel Richie, George Michael, Whitney Houston, and, of course, Michael Jackson. She'd seen their pictures on the cassette covers and in the magazines that lay scattered around the house. So she knew exactly who Mihir was talking about.

"A midget trying to reach for the moon," she said after a moment's silence, softly, tightening her lips and narrowing her eyes. "That's what you look like!"

Mihir was stunned. He couldn't say a word.

He'd been used to Moma nagging him all the time about things he did or didn't do at home. He'd been used to being told that every other boy she knew had a better job ("Look at Joe, look at Dorothy's boys!" *Dorothy's boys were in the army thanks to their father!*), and that every "young man" in church was better dressed. She nitpicked about the way Mihir walked, sat at the table, ate with his hand instead of a fork, and licked his fingers ("Disgusting!" she'd say). She even hated the way he talked. "You sound like a Bengali boy who never went to school, you know!" Things like these—always the same complaints, the same old words—had stopped bothering him a long time ago. They went in one ear and quickly out the other. *But this was something else!*

And it was not about the hair. It was about what she really thought of Mihir deep inside. Someone too small and useless and pathetic to even *look* like anybody who was not. Too small to even imitate the hairstyle of someone big! Mihir thought about the boys who paraded around the New Market area looking like Rahul Roy, or Salman Khan—*what about them?* Or the older men. Amir, the butcher, for example, and Rob Das, the second-hand record seller, who copied older heroes—Amir did Amitabh and Rob wore a Rajesh Khanna wig, and Moma knew them both. How come he'd never heard her say anything about those guys? Not a word! And she called *him* a midget. A *midget*—small body, small legs, small hands. *Small, small, small!* It was as if the ground under his feet had suddenly given way, and he was falling like a hanged man, a *small* one, a hanged dwarf, and couldn't believe it had happened to him. Mihir knew that his mother would never have told him such a thing. *Never!* Moma herself wouldn't have said this to her own son. *You don't say such things to people you love!*

For the first time in a long time, maybe four or five years, he missed his mother. He also missed his father. He imagined him stretching out his hand to ruffle his hair. *What happened to your hair?*

That deep, warm voice rang in Mihir's ears.

He slept badly. The next morning, he woke up with a headache that lasted all day, in spite of the Disprins he gulped down with tea. Moma's words kept ringing in his ears. He imagined himself as a real dwarf, like the beggar he used to be scared of as a child. Moti—he still remembered the man's name. He sat on the footpath outside their main door, and smiled and said salaam, raising his hand every time he saw Mihir and his parents. His father gave him money. Although Mihir knew Moti was not a bad man, he couldn't help being scared of him. Those big teeth in that big mouth of his, and that big head sitting on a body so small and tightly packed, like the balloon-monkeys Mihir's father used to buy for him, that his hands and legs looked like they could burst any minute. Just as the balloon-monkeys sometimes did when the balloon-wallah twisted the balloons too hard. That was what used to scare Mihir. He feared that Moti would go pop like a balloon when he smiled too hard, which he always seemed to do. Every time Mihir looked at him, he found the man smiling that way, his face like a balloon swelling from a pump's nozzle, his eyes and mouth getting bigger and bigger and bigger, forcing Mihir to look away. He had nightmares of that balloon-head popping, covering him with an ugly mess of things—Moti's big eyes and teeth dripping down his body like runny ice cream with nuts in it, still smiling at him.

Now he imagined himself as Moti. Walking around the café, taking orders and raising himself on his toes to put plates on the tables. He imagined standing next to Lambu and looking up at his face, and Ahava ruffling his curly hair and going, "I love your hair!"

The day was less busy than most Saturdays. None of the regulars showed up, at least none of those talkative ones. Mihir was glad he didn't have to worry about answering questions. "Is this a wig?" "No?" "But why did you do it?" "How much did it cost?" He didn't want to hear any compliments either. He just didn't want to hear a word about his hair, good or bad.

Luckily, CD didn't say anything. Nor did Shivshankar. They just stared, both of them. And Pappu gave a knowing smile whenever he was sure no one was watching. And Raju, as he was handing him the change for one of the first customers, asked, "Everything okay?" Very quietly, so that no one else could hear. Mihir liked that. *Sweet guy*, he thought, nodding with a smile.

Around nine in the evening, Raju told him he could leave. It was too early for a Saturday, but things were so quiet he'd already let Shiv and Dinesh go. "Nothing more will happen today," he said to Mihir. "I'll close the door in a few minutes. See you in the morning!"

A breeze was blowing. It was coming straight down Sudder Street, from the Maidan. From the river on the other side of the Maidan. Mihir remembered his father telling him that the British had left that huge area open and green so that it could work as a lung for the city. So that it could take in the air from the Ganga, and pass it on to where all the buildings were on this side of the esplanade. Right or wrong, he didn't know. But his father had been right about most things in life.

On the other side of the street, light and noise rose from the garden café of Fairlawn Hotel. He wondered if Ahava was there—he'd never managed to ask her where she was staying. A small group of backpackers stood outside the entrance to the Salvation Army guesthouse. He couldn't tell if they were waiting to get in, or if they'd come out of the building. Or if they'd just randomly stopped there, trying to figure out where they were.

Before turning left on Chowringhee Road, Mihir stopped to light a cigarette, the last of the six Flakes he'd bought in the afternoon. He edged close to the railing of the Indian Museum and turned his back to the breeze. Then striking a match, he cupped his hands, his shoulders raised and body hunched over, to keep the flame going long enough at the tip of his cigarette. It took him four attempts.

Walking past the entrance to the museum, he recognized the man sitting there with his back against the first column. The leper who sat outside Wesleyan Church on Sudder Street during the day. The man bowed, raising a fingerless hand to his forehead. Mihir dug out a few coins from one of his back pockets and dropped them in the bowl before quickly walking away. The sight of disabled beggars tortured him in a way almost nothing else did. When he was younger and believed in prayers, he prayed to God every night so that all these beggars could be healthy and whole. Maybe they wouldn't stop begging, but at least no fingerless hands and bandaged stumps for legs. No quivering body lying on the footpath, with legs that never did their job. *At least not that!*

The smoke he let out blew past a sheet of plastic tied around a couple of bars on the railing outside the art college. A loose end of the blue sheet fluttered in the breeze. For all his problems in life, Mihir thought, wasn't he luckier than that man? To be simply walking home at the end of the day? Unlike someone who couldn't either walk or had a place to go to? Wasn't he also luckier than Moti? Moma's words had made him remember that poor man. She'd made him feel like a dwarf, but he wasn't one! He didn't even *know* what it was like to be a dwarf. *A real dwarf!* To be a grown-up person trapped in a body that didn't grow. A body that scared people wherever it went, like Moti's body used to scare him!

A loud group of people walked past him, another was headed in his direction. He turned into Kyd Street, and took a few quick drags on his cigarette before flicking it away. In front of him streams of piss gleamed like tangled ribbons lying across the footpath. Mihir got off the path and took a few hurried steps down the road, then got back on it once the cloud of stench was behind him.

It was not yet ten when he reached home. Moma had already gone to bed. There was food on the table, but he felt no appetite. He removed his shoes and walked into his room as stealthily as he could. Switching on the light in his room, he sat down on the edge of the bed, his mind blank. In the mirror in front of him he could see only the top of his head, light from the table lamp next to him making it look like a knotted ball of black wool, half-buried or half-submerged. He stood up, continuing to look at the poorly-lit reflection—the head, the hair, the face, the body, the narrow shoulders and the bony arms down to the elbows. *You have the same face*, he remembered Ravi telling him. *And you can sing, too. And look at your name!* He thought about his meeting with the man tomorrow, and what he might say. Outside, the sound of a taxi followed by the tinkling of a rickshaw bell. Then another taxi. A drunk let out a shout from somewhere close to the house.

Mihir shifted his eyes from the mirror to the night table. Bending down, he took out the scissors he always kept there in the drawer. Then, looking straight at the dim reflection, he grabbed a fistful of hair with the left hand, and opened the scissors.

EPITAPH

It rained on and off through most of June and July that year. And August was full of a profusion of green the sun couldn't seem to take its eye off. Everywhere, the lushness was unrestrained. Every leaf on every tree, every blade of grass seemed determined to do its best to hide all that was broken, squalid, and ugly. Everywhere in the city there was much that was broken, squalid and ugly. And everywhere, the reckless, rainfed greenery. And the heat—the heat was inescapable. It rose daily with the sun and hung in the air long after the sun had set. Then there were days when clouds would pile up sneakily above the rooftops, and soon turn into a thick, night-black, all-covering lid over the city. Then it would pour until the whole place would look, once again, like a sad, beaten-down Venice floating in a foul sea.

It was 1995. I still remember how the late-monsoon months looked and felt that year. The color of sunlight, the play of light and shadow on everything around me, and the smell of saturation. Especially in August, especially in the days before and after the 26th, my 23rd birthday. In the dark, barely visible display case of my past, that day is like a 100-watt bulb brightening everything around it.

It was a Saturday. Niharika and I had gone to the Globe for a matinée show. And on our way there, we'd stopped at the Lower Circular Road cemetery. We'd known each other for almost three months by then, and had been out a few times before, but we'd never been to a movie together. Or a cemetery. "Who goes to a random cemetery on their birthday?" my friend Timir had said when I told him about the trip the next day. He was an ex-Naxal, and called himself a failed revolutionary. "Celebrating birthdays and going to cemeteries— bourgeois sentimentality at its most pathetic!" He shook his head as he threw fistfuls of wheat at his pet pigeons in the courtyard. The pigeons flapped their wings and pecked away at the grains like they hadn't been fed before. "It's infantile!" He threw more wheat, stirring his pigeons into a feeding frenzy, and shook his head again. I wasn't sure who he disapproved of this time—me or the pigeons. It was my first birthday since getting to know Niharika, so our meeting that day was special in a way none of our previous meetings had been. *Who cared what we did or where we went!* The important thing was that I was with her the whole day, which hadn't happened before. Timir didn't care about *that*. The man was almost thirteen years older, and we didn't see eye to eye on many things. But I admired him; he was different from everyone I knew. My mother, a card-carrying member of the Communist Party of India (Marxist), never liked him much. Although she never said why, I had a feeling it was because of their ideological rivalry—moderate left (my mother) versus extreme left (Timir). But she never stopped me from being close to the man.

Niharika and her parents lived in an old house on Circus Avenue. Her mother had asked me to eat lunch with them. She'd cooked my favorite mutton rezala as a birthday treat and Niharika had baked a cake. "Here, a bit more," her mother would say and ladle more food onto my plate. "I've made it for you. Don't be shy!" By the time the cake was put on the table, I couldn't eat anymore, and promised to come back for it the next day.

I felt so bloated after that, I wanted to walk. We were waiting for a bus at a stop near her house. The ride was going to take between ten and fifteen minutes depending on the traffic, and the walk to Globe wouldn't take more than twenty-five minutes, and we had almost an hour and a half in hand. "Let's do it," Niharika said, even though the sun was scorching and we *hated* walking these streets with all the dust, smoke and traffic noise.

I don't remember exactly what had made us walk into the cemetery. After hurrying across the Park Street-AJC Bose Road crossing we'd resumed our leisurely pace. The footpath was uneven with bricks jutting out in places and muddy water collected in troughs of all shapes and sizes. Niharika was careful with every step, walking around piles of rubble that could either hurt her feet or get her brown leather sandals dirty. Ahead of us, we noticed a sheet of black tarpaulin covering a bit of the footpath against the cemetery wall. It was like a poorly made tent. A pair of feet stuck out of its opening, which was blocked by a wheelbarrow. Walking past the tent we heard someone snoring inside. Then we stood facing the entrance to the cemetery. *Was it my idea to walk in?* Or was it hers? It's possible that, both of us were so attracted by the sight of all those big trees in there and the large areas of shade under them, we'd walked in without even discussing the matter. Plus, we had time to kill.

The place was quiet and empty. A warm, moist smell of vegetation hung in the air. There were smells of flowers that I both recognized and didn't. Mangy dogs panted in the shade of trees and cats slept in damp gutters. "Look," Niharika said, pointing at a few vultures and crows. They were scavenging the undergrowth close to the boundary wall on the other side. *A dead cat or a dog*, I thought, but didn't say that to her. The sound of traffic on AJC Bose Road seemed somewhat muffled by the wall and the trees inside the cemetery. We found a middle-aged couple standing statue-like next to a new grave, a garish sign on the stonework reading *Ghulam & Sons*. I remember finding that interesting—a Muslim name in a Christian cemetery. Niharika said something about how sad the couple looked. An old woman sat on the edge of another tomb, not as new as the first one, but well looked after. She had three or four mongrels for company. She didn't look particularly sad. Not only that, I thought I'd even heard her sing. "Did you hear that?" I asked Niharika. She said she hadn't; she was thinking about the couple.

An odd sense of sadness infused the thrill of our date. We walked side by side between rows of graves. We held hands, letting go only to take a closer look at old tombs. We bent low to inspect their crumbling, moss-covered surface and read whatever was legible on the headstones. Both of us liked doing that, we discovered—reading epitaphs. Then we found one with the name Edgar Hill, who'd been buried there in June, 1854.

1854! I remember reading the year again and again, trying to grasp just how far back in time that was, and wondering what the place might have looked like back then. He'd been shot by the police, the inscription said. I wondered how many people might have come to his funeral. And who they might have been. Maybe just the undertakers, a couple of policemen and a priest. And maybe his wife, too, if he was married. Or his fiancée, if he had one. I wondered what the whole place might have looked like. Certainly not as many graves, and there must have been fields all around, and goats and cows grazing in them. Clumps of trees dotting the landscape, and huddles of huts here and there and big colonial buildings towering over them, and a church or two. Horses and horse-drawn carriages on dirt roads. And people going about their daily lives—the natives in cotton dhotis and saris and the English in their three-piece suits and silk dresses and bonnets. Just like in the paintings and drawings of old Calcutta. It was the exact same place where I was, but another world! *And it was June*, I thought, so the monsoon might already have started. I imagined a dark dome of clouds overhead, and the sound of shovels hitting Edgar Hill's coffin in pouring rain.

"God, just twenty-five!" Niharika said.

"Only two years older than me!"

"Who knows when the family found out back in Canterbury!"

"If they ever did."

"Who knows why they killed him!"

I tore a tuft of dried-up fern from the foot of the headstone, which tilted to a side with most of the tomb having sunk into the earth. "No one probably looked at it in a hundred years!"

"Poor Edgar Hill," she said.

Minutes later, still standing in front of that grave we kissed each other for the first time. "Many happy returns of the day," Niharika had whispered.

"Your birthday reminds me of Edgar Hill," she wrote to me in a letter in 2004, a few days before my birthday that year. "I remember the epitaph—*Edgar Albert Hill of Canterbury, born 1829, shot by the police the 1st of June 1854*. Then it says, *Forget not the faithful dead*." I found the letter between the pages of a book I hadn't touched in years. Written on both sides of a single sheet of paper, the paper yellowed, the ink slightly faded. "Pay him a visit some time," it says. "For memory's sake."

A few months after hearing about Edgar Hill's grave, Timir had surprised me by suggesting I take him there. "You said the man had been shot and killed by the police, right?" He said he too had come close to being killed by police. "Very close," he said. "It's a miracle I'm alive." He wasn't for too long after that, dying of a heart attack early next year. We never managed to visit Edgar Hill's grave.

I miss the man. I miss the warmth of that selfless concern for others he seemed to generate without effort. A side of him my mother never got to see thanks to their ideological difference. In my memory he feeds his pigeons and talks about right and wrong in that prickly way he always did. *You took a bit too long to grow up*, I imagine him saying about me not celebrating my birthdays anymore. It stopped with my mother's death seven years ago.

The monsoon has had a slow start this year. Not much rain in June, although July was better. And there's been a lot of scattered clouds and haze of late. There was an early-evening thunderstorm day before yesterday. The same has been forecast for today, August 26, 2016, and the temperature in the middle 30s with high humidity. The same story as the one back in 1995, except for the greenery—the lack of it. It doesn't cover the squalor it once did.

It's a few minutes after five when I leave my office. The walk to the Park Street-AJC Bose Road crossing takes me less than 10 minutes. I remember the spot where Niharika and I had stood on the other side of the intersection, needing to cross Park Street. Hurrying across AJC Bose Road I think of that letter of hers: "I'll live the rest of my life thinking how different it all could have been...."

Inside the cemetery things look a bit more disheveled than before, and not as green. The smell in the air is of heat, parched earth and dry grass, not the damp aroma of foliage and flowers that I remember. I look left and right trying to get my bearings. I cannot see anyone, and hear anything but the traffic noise and the cawing of crows and the flapping of their wings as they fly from one tree to another, and the rustle of sapless twigs. I get off the wide central path on the left side and walk seventy or eighty feet along the length of the cemetery, looking at the graves on both sides, and also at the boundary wall both in front of me and behind to see if I can remember the location of Edgar Hill's grave in relation to the surroundings. I walk around reading headstones that look vaguely familiar, wiping the sweat off my face every few minutes with my rolled-up shirtsleeves.

After some time, I walk back to the entrance, turn around, and stand there trying to call up the images from twenty-one years ago and compare them with what's in front of me. And what's in front of me looks slightly more derelict, and at the same time, flashier in places. More graves with railings around them now, it seems. From one on my left with the metalwork painted parrot green, a crow watches me. It lifts off as I start walking back into the cemetery and then alights on the same spot as I pass the tomb.

Who am I doing this for? I think to myself. *And for what?* I have no idea where Niharika is. I haven't heard from her since that letter in 2004. And Timir, who wanted me to bring him here, has been dead for years. There's absolutely no one I can share this experience with. No one I can talk to about this solo trip to the cemetery on my birthday, and this obsessive, meaningless search, which is sure to end in futility now that the clouds are beginning to stack up in a corner of the sky, and I can hear the rumble of thunder.

Too many crows, it suddenly occurs to me. They're swooping down from the trees, the rooftops behind the cemetery, sitting on headstones, and cawing nonstop. The tomb in front of me looks like it could be the one. If memory serves, this is where Niharika and I had stood kissing. But I'm not sure, and there's no way I can read the marker thanks to the overgrown weeds. I crouch down, trying to remove some of the covering of dried-up moss and fern. As I pull out a tuft of tall grass, three lizards scurry out, and there's a ripple in the bush at the other end of the grave. There's no telling if it's a snake!

The rumble of thunder sounds a lot closer now and the sky is almost half covered with clouds. *That's it*, I whisper to myself. Getting to my feet I see something move out of the corner of my eye—a human head rising slowly from behind a tall gravestone on my right, roughly fifteen feet from where I am. I let out a terrified scream. I had no idea there was anyone sitting there, and so close to me! A man with matted hair and beard, his face frozen in a silent laugh.

He comes out from behind the gravestone and shuffles past me, then he turns right, going not toward the gate but in the opposite direction, further into the graveyard. Soaked in sweat, my heart pounding, I take a few steps toward the gravestone behind which the man was sitting. There's food scattered all over the tomb—two crows and a sparrow pecking busily at rice, pieces of bread, fishbone.

A clap of thunder makes the birds fly away. I keep standing there, as if unable to move. And the first drops of rain begin to fall.

RAIN

It's the first day of monsoon. From where he's sitting in the teashop, Tuhin can see scarves of rain wrapping and unwrapping themselves around a street lamp on the other side of the road. The stronger the gusts of wind the thicker the sheets of rain, making the lamp look like a giant candy floss with an angry, swirling head—swelling and shrinking, and swelling again. Every now and then, a flash of lightning and a deafening clap of thunder, the men in the shop screaming: *Bring it on, bring it on!*

A fresh gust carries a fine spray deep into the shop, covering everything. Which no one seems to mind. Tuhin doesn't either. It's a welcome respite after days of oppressive heat melted the tar on roads, made the cold drink sellers run out of their stock, and the mentally deranged turn rabid.

The two men Tuhin is sharing the table with are talking about one such person. They sent him to fetch paan. "He scared me!" one of them says. "A week ago, I wouldn't have gone within ten feet of him." "It's the heat!" the other one says. "The last few days were really bad, but he's so much better today. An hour of rain and he's already a different man."

The man returns with paan wrapped in plantain leaf. He's completely drenched in spite of the umbrella he carried. He hands the wet bundle and some change to the older of the two men, who presses a coin into his hand and says, "One-rupee profit from one-rupee business. Not bad, no?" "Not bad at all!" The man laughs, his teeth stained with betel juice and nicotine. He folds the umbrella, which belongs to one of these men, and lays it down on the floor. Then with a quick wave of his hand he goes back into the pouring rain, humming a song.

The two men laugh, mouths full of paan.

Laltu, the teashop owner, squeezes himself past Tuhin's chair and bends over to reach a calendar lying on the floor behind him. It's a picture of Kali, blue face with a garland of golden-yellow hibiscus. The wind has blown it off the peg on the wall. "When did it happen?" one of the paan-chewing men says. "Who knows!" his companion replies. "We were too lost in idle chatter. Forgive us, Ma!" He touches his bowed forehead with the tips of his palms, eyes closed. Laltu does the same after putting the calendar back on the wall.

Kali's tongue is wavy, soaked with rain water.

"Any place left?" a man calls from the door, his umbrella still open, blocking the view of the street lamp. Laltu points to the chair next to Tuhin's, the only one available. "Aare, where have you been all this time?" someone says to the newcomer. Tuhin moves his feet to avoid the rivulets flowing in from all the umbrellas left at the door. The chair next to him is slightly damp, which the man notices but sits down anyway. "Will tell you later," he says raising his voice, and then orders his tea. "Without sugar, okay?" he says to Laltu.

When Tuhin came here forty-five minutes ago, it was a quieter place. The rain had already started, but it was not too strong and people were still out and about. There were only five or six people inside. Now it's full, and noisy. Which he doesn't like, but he doesn't know where else to go.

He doesn't want to go home, at least not yet. There isn't much left of it anyway—*home*. Not after what happened last night. He wonders if he could've done something about it—the way things changed, on his watch. If he should've put his foot down, and done it at the right time to keep things from sliding out of control. He wonders if that could have made things go back to the way they were during their almost year-long courtship, and the first two-plus years of marriage.

The noise reminds Tuhin of the fish market he goes to every Sunday morning. It's less than a hundred meters from where he's now, and five to six minutes' walk from their flat. A perpetually wet and muddy place even in dry weather, reeking of fish and fish blood. And always noisy. He hates the place as much as he hates fish, and goes there only for Uma. Who cannot do without fish, but faints at the thought of buying it herself. "Eeeshh!" she'd make a face if Tuhin ever asked her to do it. "Do it *once*," he'd urge her sometimes. "For a change!" "I'd much rather give up fish!" she'd respond. She doesn't touch meat, eggs, or dairy, and the beans and pulses aren't her things either. So, on his weekly trip to the bazar, after he's done buying vegetables and some mutton for himself from Karim, the butcher who sits next to the rice vendors with two or three skinned goat carcasses hanging from the rafter of his stall, Tuhin goes to the smelliest and noisiest part of the market to pick up fish for Uma.

Another gust of rain blows into the shop, wetting Tuhin and the other men at the table. The calendar behind him scrapes the wall. "You're totally wet now," one of the paan-chewing men says to the one sitting next to Tuhin. "What can be done?" the man shrugs, taking a sip of his tea. "God only knows what would've happened to West Bengal if it weren't for the communists!" Tuhin hears someone say. Then there's a blinding flash of lightning, quickly followed by a thunderclap. "The state would have prospered," a younger man responds after the sound of thunder dies down. "And we would've had jobs!" "But without the communists, the Hindus and Muslims would be at one another's throats, like they're everywhere else in the country," the first one counters. "Don't forget *that*!"

The voices of these two men and those of others, and the sound of clapping hands, laughter, coughs and sneezes, the clink of glasses and kettles, and the hiss of the gas stove begin to sound like a clump of noise worms writhing in Tuhin's ears. He motions Laltu to give him another tea, and looks out at the candy-floss street lamp.

The thoughts of last night come back to him.

He'd been itching to light a cigarette but didn't, knowing it wouldn't be wise. He peed standing only inches from the wall to make sure there was no noise, his feet wide apart to keep the shoes from getting wet. Wiping his hands on the pants, he switched on the phone to see if someone had tried to call. He was expecting to hear from Amsterdam about a passenger's missing suitcase. It hadn't been loaded onto the plane that arrived last night. There were no missed calls. He switched off the phone and slipped it back into his pocket.

The air was still, heavy with heat.

A stir in the hibiscus bush startled him. It was a cat, one of a dozen or so that prowl around the house every day. In the half-light, he could see it pause for a moment, turning its head to study him carefully, before slinking away. He imagined the questioning look in its eyes. *What do you think you're doing here?* he imagined it thinking, if cats could think. He had no idea if they could or not; he couldn't care less.

He'd been standing there for almost an hour, swatting mosquitoes that flew into his face or bit the exposed parts of his arms, waving away the ones buzzing in his ears. When his knees hurt, he squatted for a few minutes. Every now and then, as lights from the flats above partly lit up the passage, Tuhin ducked behind the bush. He was glad the passage was meant only for them. A high wall separates it from the parking area, which leads to the stairs to the upper floors. It's this sense of privacy that had made them choose this flat over the one on the 2nd floor, which was bigger and had the same rent. Here, they could walk around naked with the windows open. They could be as naughty and loud as they pleased, without fearing people might hear them.

Around half past seven, he heard a taxi stop outside the gate. It was Uma. He *knew* she would return early because he'd told her he might run late. He'd lied.

Tuhin kept standing at the far end of the passage, which ends abruptly with a wall separating the building from the backyard of the one behind. A strong smell of rotting garbage rose from there. He wished the gardenias along the side of their passage had been in bloom instead of the scentless hibiscus.

The moon broke through the clouds for a minute or two. A bunch of crows suddenly started to caw. They roost on a big tree across the street—ten or fifteen of them, maybe more. Sometimes they caw in the middle of the night, which gets the dogs going.

Above his head, the back of their living room AC started to hum. There was an unusual urgency in the sound of Uma's flipflops as she walked in and out of the room. He heard doors open and close, and wondered if the AC in the bedroom had also been turned on. He heard the toilet being flushed and the shower started. She was in a hurry.

Less than half an hour later, Noel arrived.

She'd brought him home for the first time four or five months ago. They had met at some work-related party, and he'd offered to give her a ride home. Opening the door that night, Tuhin had found a radiant Uma standing with a tall, well-dressed man. Her small, slender body rippled with an energy he hadn't seen in her for a long time. Her eyes shone. "Noel, this is Tuhin, my husband," she'd said. Tuhin had shaken hands with Noel Ananthan, a Citi Bank manager, and asked him in for a cup of tea.

In the months that followed, Uma's world spun like its center of gravity had shifted. Or *he* had been flung out of his place there. She didn't tire of talking about Noel. *Can you tell from his looks he's half English? That his mother was white? She died a few years ago. He grew up mostly in India, though. In Madras and Delhi, and then went to university in the UK. Oxford? Cambridge? One of those, I forget which. Can you tell he's thirty-nine?*

Tuhin couldn't tell the man was thirty-nine, or that his mother was white. He didn't give a shit, either.

He could hear them walk into the living room now. She'd worn a sari to work; he wondered what she'd changed into. She offered to make tea or coffee. The man asked for water. "Too hot for tea and coffee," he said. "Lemonade?" Uma asked. "Just water please," he said.

By the end of winter, Tuhin had got used to him calling almost every evening. Every time her phone squeaked with an incoming SMS, he could tell from the look on her face if it was from him. Mostly, it was. The attention with which she read his messages, and punched in her replies, was itself a form of betrayal. It was as if her handset was an extension of the man, and she'd go on pecking and caressing it, sometimes for as long as an hour. The smile on her face would make Tuhin walk away from where she was.

Gone was the time when he called her at home Saturday nights, when he wasn't too busy at the airport. She would ask him if things were under control at work, if the flight was on time. She'd ask if he was smoking too many cigarettes, or having too much coffee. And he'd ask her about the show she might be watching on TV. They would make their Sunday plans—would they eat out? Where would they go? Should he make a reservation? Or would she do that? What was she wearing? *Was it sexy enough?* They'd go on in that vein until Tuhin had to get back to work.

Now she was rarely at home Saturday nights. *This event, that event*—business dinner, party, baby shower. No shortage of reasons for her to be away from home and return late, sometimes *after* him. And the nights she was at home, he feared she might not be alone. It was his *fear*. He wasn't sure. It was just this nagging suspicion that had taken hold of him since that phone call one Saturday evening in early February. The hint of surprise in her voice when she answered, and the lack of interest. Was that because she had company? *Was Noel there with her?* Could he ask her? What would it mean if he did? And what would he say if she wanted know *why* he was asking? Maybe she wasn't surprised at all, and didn't even sound like she was. Maybe it was all his imagination, warped by the sudden changes in her social life. That it got busier might have nothing to do with Noel. And that day, she might simply have been too tired to talk. Too tired even to tell him that she didn't have the energy to talk, and just waited for him to hang up.

"If you're suspicious of your wife, you're already divorced from her," he'd heard his mother say once while talking to Uma. They hadn't been married yet. "That's emotional divorce!" she'd added. "Who's suspicious of whom?" Tuhin wanted to know. "None of your business," his mother had told him with a slap on his wrist.

Tuhin had stopped calling Uma Saturday evenings. Even during the week, if he needed to say something before returning home, he'd send an SMS. They talked on the phone only when she called him. On the face of it, it was a small shift in the way they did things. So small that Tuhin wasn't even sure she noticed. The needle, the visible part of it, had moved only a little, but its hidden tail had covered a whole arc in his mind. He never found out whom his mother had meant when she talked about emotional divorce. He wondered what she'd say if she knew what was going on with him. He wondered if he should talk to her about it.

Some nights, he caught a whiff of cigarette smoke and perfumes when he came home. She'd say it was her colleagues. Mita, Anupama, Abhirup, Purnima, Dhruv, Shefali, Rakesh—any two or three of them, every few days. *But not Noel.* Which made him think he might really have been wrong, his fears merely those of a jealous husband—completely baseless.

The door to the first-floor balcony opened. Biswanath Guha, who lives upstairs with his wife, came out and lit a cigarette. He stood there humming a song between puffs, a part of his shadow on the passage. Crouched behind the hibiscus bush, Tuhin shivered in the heat, his heart racing. Somewhere close by, two cats started to fight. "Hey, huut!" Biswanath Guha clapped his hands to shoo them away. "Close the door," his wife screamed from inside. They scream at each other all the time, the two of them. "Will we fight like them when we get old?" Uma asked him once. "If we do enough of something else, we won't," he'd said. "Let me show you what that is!" Laughing, she'd run away from the bedroom. He'd chased her down in the kitchen.

The man upstairs flicked his cigarette into the dark, and went back into the flat. After he closed the door, Tuhin came out from behind the bush. Holding his breath, he tiptoed to the window with bent knees.

Silence.

He couldn't hear anything at all. It couldn't be taking her *that* long to get a glass of water from the kitchen. Was she making something for him? A sandwich? *Was the man sitting there by himself?*

A mosquito landed on Tuhin's right cheek, instantly plunging its stinger into him. He held still, not swatting or waving it away. Barely breathing, he inched closer to the window, and placed his left ear against its rough wood. A sign—*any sign*—to dispel his fears, to prove his suspicions wrong. He let the mosquito have its fill.

Someone upstairs started to blow a conch shell. It was Mrs. Guha, doing the ritual emptying of her gigantic lungs into the conch—one, two, three unendingly long times. It was the hum of the AC that he heard as soon as she stopped. Then Uma's breath, the shortness of it. The way she breathes every time they kiss hard.

It stopped, then started again. Quick and heavy.

Tuhin walked away from the window with a pounding chest, his ears hot. Touching a spot on his right cheek, he felt something on his fingertips. Something damp and grainy. He wiped his fingers on the gate, as he opened it to step out onto the street.

A wrinkled saffron crust has formed on the tea. Tuhin held the glass in his hand, without taking a single sip. He throws his head back to swallow the thick, cold liquid in one gulp, hoping no one notices him.

"Aren't you tired of talking politics all the time?" the man next to Tuhin says to the loudest man in the teashop, the communist party supporter. A thin, bald man in his late sixties wearing glasses with thick black frames. "Why just politics?" he responds cheerfully. "I can talk about anything. Cricket, East Bengal, Mohun Bagan, cinema, Satyajit Ray—you name it. I read four newspapers daily, my friend. *Four!* Two Bengali and two English. Front to back. Including the crosswords and comics."

"And the matrimonial columns?" someone asks with a mischievous laugh. "Those too. For folks like you. In case you're planning a second round!"

As most of the shop roars with laughter, Tuhin rises from his chair. Paying for his tea, he steps outside and quickly takes shelter under the projected roof of the grocery store next door. He inserts himself into the crowd of partly wet bodies waiting for the rain to let up.

An empty bus drives past, sending waves of muddy water to the steps where they're standing. Loud voices and peals of laughter spill out of the teashop.

He hasn't had any contact with Uma since last night. He'd texted her to let her know he would spend the night at Deepak's. "OK," she'd written back. He wonders if she's at home now.

As soon as the rain eases a little, the crowd starts to thin. Tuhin waits for another ten or fifteen minutes. Then he rolls up his pants, takes off the shoes, and steps into the ankle-deep water.

In front of him, the road is like a shallow canal lit up by occasional flashes of lightning, thunder rumbling in the distance. He thinks of the madman, the way he walked in the rain humming a song.

By the time Tuhin reaches home, he's soaked to the skin, and doesn't mind that he is.

I CAN BE HIS PROXY

"Someone called!" the note said. Just those two words and the exclamation mark. It was on the Cipla notepad in the middle of the table. Anjan knew the handwriting. It was Sundar's—he was into exclamation marks. He hadn't bothered to peel the note off the pad and put it on Anjan's side of the table. But since they were the only ones who sat here, it couldn't be for anyone else. Ranja and Sudip, who worked part time, shared the other table.

Who could it be?

Not too many people had his office number, and Sundar knew most of them. His mother was the one who called most frequently, but never this early. Also, they were together until he left home an hour and a half ago.

Enough! he thought. He wouldn't spend a minute more worrying about it. Whoever had called, would call back if it was urgent. Besides, Sundar would be back from the tea stall any minute now. He was always the first one to arrive. He'd drop his bag on the floor near his chair, open the window next to their table, and go out again for a glass of tea. He went to this makeshift place about three hundred meters from the office. He did it every day, before starting the day's work. It was a ritual he couldn't do without.

Anjan wished both he and Sundar had mobile phones. He could find out right away who'd called. In fact, he wouldn't even be in this situation if he had a device like that. "Buy a mobile," Bhaskar had told him many times. "We're more than half a decade into the new millennium, you cannot *not* have a mobile phone." Bhaskar worked for The Statesman, and had one. "I'm not as mobile as you," Anjan would tell him. "You need one anyway," Bhaskar argued. "It will define how you live your life going forward. Having a mobile, or not, will make all the difference."

Anjan wasn't convinced. He couldn't afford one either. The senior artist's salary in the design department of this export house was barely enough to pay the bills. Without his mother's pension, they'd be hand-to-mouth.

It was nine fifty. Sundar wasn't back yet, which was unusual. If he had to go somewhere else, he would've left a message saying so. The sheep-leather swatches they'd worked on two days ago had to be sorted by size and design before Anjan could start putting the finishing touches. Sundar had told him yesterday that he would do it before leaving the office. It was his job as a junior artist. He did all the prep work, and did it fairly well for the most part. "I'm staying a bit longer today," he'd said. "I'll do the sorting last."

He hadn't. He hadn't even tidied up his side of the table, which was also unusual given how fussy he was. His side was always spick and span. Unlike Anjan's, which was cluttered with magazines, pencils, pens, brushes, paint bottles, ink pots, erasures, design reference books, old bills, notepads, and who knew what else.

He felt hot, the back of his shirt still soaked with sweat. He rose from his chair to reach the fan regulator on the switchboard behind him. As soon as he increased the fan's speed, pieces of paper started to fly away from the table. He went around the room to collect them one by one—a voucher, three order slips, a tracing sheet, an A4 with scribbles and doodles, and a few scraps of useless paper, one of which was an old counterpart of a New Empire Cinema ticket.

Anjan wondered if he should walk to the tea stall to see what the matter was. He realized that he hadn't yet managed to get any work done. The pile of swatches lay exactly where and how he'd found it. He'd picked up a piece with the floral motif—three roses with stems and leaves, several blades of grass and a butterfly—but couldn't focus on it. The thought of the phone call kept getting in the way, and Sundar's unusual absence.

Every few minutes, he glanced at the note. As if reading those two words over and over would reveal more of their meaning. He stared at the blankness around the writing, the way it wrapped itself around the two words and the exclamation mark. He felt drawn toward blank spaces, and liked using them in his own work—not what he did for the export house, but in his paintings and drawings, whatever they were worth (which, he knew in his heart of hearts, was *nothing*). He liked leaving a lot of space around the areas of interest. "Why do you keep doing that?" Bhaskar would ask. Anjan never had a good answer. He just couldn't help painting that way, that was all. Bhaskar reviewed art exhibitions; he knew far more about art, and pretty much everything else, than Anjan did. There was no way he could defend his paintings against Bhaskar's criticisms. Besides, wasn't defending one's own art a bit like having to defend how one's home looked? You arranged your possessions the way you liked. Put things in places where you wanted them put. What was the point of justifying the placement of your chair, table, bookshelf, bed? The pictures that hung on your walls—if they did—and how they did. You put them where you put them based on your taste—your own sense of balance and harmony—to make you feel at home. If it was someone else's home, they'd do it differently. They'd have a different arrangement of things, which themselves might look different—different shapes, sizes, colors, and so on. Painting, for Anjan, was like that. Each piece was an effort to quench the thirst of *his* eyes—he painted for himself, not for anyone else. The lines, the shapes, the layers of color, the light and shadow, and the empty spaces between and around the painted areas—they all strove to create something on the paper (it was mostly paper; he couldn't afford canvas) for something in him to say, *Yes, that's how I like it!* Simple thing—no need of any clever arguments to back it up. *I love blank spaces! That's why I keep doing that. Do I ask you why your desk is so close to your bed? Why your bookshelf is where it is? Your choice, right? Same here. My art is my home, whether you like it or not.* He couldn't say any of this to Bhaskar. He was terrified of clever arguments.

He glanced at the note once again. *Someone called!*

The swatch was still in his hands. He laid it flat on the table and ran his right palm across it, from right to left and back. He did it several times, feeling the grain of the leather. He thought about all the work that needed to be done to meet the shipping deadline. There were footsteps outside the door. *At last*, he thought, and looked at his watch. It was nine minutes to twelve. Ranja walked in. Unlike Sudip, she was always on time.

Ranja!

The fan pulled some of the hot, humid air from outside and swirled it around the room along with her perfume. "Hi," she said, hanging her purse from the back of her chair. "You're alone today?" He'd spent the last two hours waiting for Sundar, but was glad it was Ranja instead of him. She had on an off-white cotton sari—she hardly wore anything other than saris, and they were always cotton. "Yes," he said. She turned to look at the table. The buttoned back of her blouse was soaked with sweat. Its shallow drop of buttons and the narrow back strap of her bra standing out like a plus sign. A bit of her bobbed hair stuck to the damp nape of her neck. "Sundar's note says I need to do the small swatches?" She turned around. "But they're not sorted," he said. "No problem," she said, walking over to Anjan's table.

Her nearness paralyzed him. As she collected the smaller swatches, carefully separating them from the bigger ones—the fluid, graceful movement of her hands, her body bending ever so close—Anjan sank into her scent like a pebble dropped in a pond.

He poured himself another glass of water. One of the people that had his number, whom Sundar didn't know, was Bankim Manna. Renuka's husband. He'd called only once, and Anjan had picked up the phone himself. He'd asked the two of them not to call unless it was absolutely necessary, as it had been that one time when Manna-da had called. (He called him Manna-da because Pijush, his friend who'd introduced him to the man—they were colleagues—called him that. Besides, he was at least ten years older.) Could *he* be the "someone" of the note? *And what if he was?* What could have made him call this time? Was it yesterday? After he left work? Sundar had said he'd stay a bit longer. Or was it earlier today? There was no way to tell. That one time when he'd called, Anjan was alone in the office. Sudip had just stepped out. It was a Tuesday. Sundar was on leave that week. The final monthly consignment had been dispatched the week before, so there was hardly any work at all. Anjan had planned to visit Renuka at the hospital. She'd been in labor for several hours. Manna-da had called to ask if he could get there as soon as possible.

The baby was already there by the time Anjan had reached the hospital. It was a girl. They'd put her in the ICU because of some complications. It had been a difficult pregnancy; Renuka had all kinds of problems. The two of them had to stay in the hospital for almost two weeks. Manna-da never called after that, even though Renuka and her daughter (they named her Bidisha; he liked the name) had been unwell several times. In the first four or five months, he'd gone to their house a few times—maybe three times, if he remembered correctly. He visited them again when Bidisha turned one. After that, he never went to their house. And the last time he'd seen the man was months ago, shortly before his abrupt resignation. He'd gone to his office to return a book he'd lent to Anjan.

The Ascetic of Desire. Not a book he'd ever pick up on his own. Books didn't interest him unless they were about art, and had lots of images—pictures of paintings and drawings. Like the fat coffee table books that he always looked at but couldn't afford to buy. "Have you read this one?" Manna-da pushed it toward him across the table. This was only their seventh or eighth meeting. He'd come to Pijush's office at the State Central Library in Ultadanga, which wasn't far from his own office. They had plans of going somewhere for an after-work drink.

They'd been doing this a couple of times a month since Pijush moved back to Calcutta two years ago. Anjan would come to SCL, and then they'd take a bus to Dharmatala and get into one of their three favorite joints—Duke, Saqi, and Chhota Bristol. Not the nicest of places, but they were cheap, especially Chhota Bristol. Once in a while, if they had a bit of extra cash and wanted to have a bite, they went to Chung Wah.

Pijush had gone upstairs to see someone and had asked Manna-da to keep Anjan company. He and Pijush had known each other since high school. In many ways, he felt closer to him than to Bhaskar, who was all about books and ideas, which intimidated him. Pijush, on the other hand, didn't care about books even though he worked in a library. He handled them the way a cashier handled cash—just keeping track of things as they entered the library (the cash drawer for the cashier); each item as valuable as the next. And he didn't have a mobile phone either. "It's a novel about Vatsayana," Manna-da said. "You know who Vatsayana was, right?" *Of course!* Who didn't? "It's my personal copy—you can have it." Manna-da smiled with a slight nod.

A novel! Anjan wouldn't have minded looking at a copy of *Kama Sutra*, but who cared about a novel about its author? "Read it and let me know what you think." No one had ever asked Anjan to do such a thing. Not even Bhaskar.

Ranja had arrived less than an hour ago and had already completed more than a dozen pieces. He could see the bunch of finished swatches getting bigger on the right side of her table. As for him, he'd finished only one drawing—nothing having to do with office work, but a back portrait of her. He did it whenever he was alone in the office while she worked, sitting the way she was sitting now. The head tilted left, the slender neck, the left shoulder a bit higher than the right, the long arms, one elbow planted on the table, the other moving. And the heart-stopping plunge of her back into her heart-stopping waist. He loved the way the tip of his HB felt against the paper's tooth, the sweet swish it made as it created a version of her on the paper. Every time he had a chance, he'd take out his sketchbook from the locked drawer and capture these details as faithfully as he could. And as *quickly* as he could. The sneakiness made him feel like he was a street photographer, stealing candid shots of unsuspecting subjects.

Bhaskar hated street photographers; he called them voyeurs. If he saw Anjan now, who knew what he'd say.

He was in the middle of his second sketch when the phone rang, startling him. He closed the sketchbook hastily and picked it up. It was his mother. "Have you eaten?" *The same question, every day!* "Not yet," Anjan said. "Busy right now!"

They'd gone to Duke that day. Anjan showed the book to Pijush. "Manna-da gave it to me when I was waiting for you," he said. Pijush glanced at the cover as he poured beer into his glass. He wiped his fingers on his pants and picked it up. He turned the front cover, then the back. "Hm," he said, "it's not ours." "No," Anjan said, "he said it's his personal copy." Pijush handed it back to Anjan and picked up his beer. "Cheers," he said. "Cheers," Anjan said, putting the book away.

After years in the North Bengal State Library in Cooch Behar, Pijush was happy he'd got that job in Calcutta. He was happy to be back. There was no place he liked more than this city, and few things more than spending time with his old classmate. They'd gone to different colleges—Anjan to the Indian Art College, and he to Scottish Church. Then he went to Durgapur for three years before moving to Cooch Behar. Anjan hadn't gone anywhere, moving hopelessly from one low-paying ad-agency job in the city to another, while trying his luck with various art galleries. "We have to make up for lost time," Pijush said. Anjan couldn't agree more.

A month or so later, on a Saturday, he went to Pijush's office to find that he'd just left for home. "His father is unwell," Manna-da said. "Nothing serious, but his mother wanted him to go home. He called your office to let you know, but no one answered. Maybe you were already on the way. He said he'd call you on Monday." As Anjan was about to leave, the man said, "But I can be his proxy, if you don't mind. Unless you have other plans, of course. I do drink a beer now and then." *Fine, but please no discussion about Vatsayana*, Anjan wanted to tell him. He hadn't read the book, and didn't want Manna-da to bring it up.

He didn't. He talked about a woman instead, whom he wanted Anjan to meet. *His own wife*, as it turned out. Renuka.

Long story short—Manna-da didn't have a brother, and was desperate to have a son of his own. He didn't want to be *the last branch* of his family tree. *Who would conduct his last rites then?* That they couldn't have a child was, of course, his wife's fault. Until medical exams proved that there was nothing wrong with her. His low sperm count was the culprit. He was devastated. He was so close to going completely bonkers, that he had to go to a counselor. Finally, after nine years of marriage, countless trips to gynecologists, ayurvedic and Tibetan doctors, sadhus, pirs and palmists, and wearing fistfuls of gems and talismans wherever on the body one could wear them, they decided to look for a different kind of help. "There's nothing wrong with it," he'd told his wife, who didn't like the idea of having someone else's child. She'd found the solution morally degrading. "What about artificial insemination?" Manna-da had argued. "Isn't it the same thing? Women abroad do it all the time!" When Renuka suggested they adopt a boy instead, he said at least one of them should be the child's biological parent. Then she gave in. And agreed to see *this nice, young artist.*

"No need to tell Pijush any of this, by the way," Manna-da said.

The phone rang, startling Anjan once again. It was his boss this time. Barun Deb, the owner of Deb Exports. "Sundar's wife is sick, that's why he couldn't come today," he said. "She had to be hospitalized last night. I'm sorry I forgot to let you know earlier. But Ranja is there, isn't she? If the swatches are ready, you can send them to the fabricators." "They're not," Anjan said. "No problem, we have time," Barun Deb said before hanging up.

"They *are* ready!" Ranja smiled, walking to his table with the bunch of finished swatches. He glanced at his sketchpad to make sure it wasn't open. "At least the smaller ones," she said, setting the bunch gently down on his table. Anjan could hear his heart pounding inside his chest. Could he get any closer to her? Could anyone *help* in any way? Ranja lingered there for a moment, as did the smile on her face. As if she knew what was going on.

He looked at her work—the top piece of the bunch that she'd just put on the table. How good she was at what she did! How clean and well-defined her lines were, how precise the application of color. She had a BFA from Rabindra Bharati, and it showed. And her *real* work, her paintings—he'd been to two of her shows—were on an entirely different level. Unlike him, she painted large canvases, which filled the gallery walls. Which the gallery owners liked. He did too. "Scale matters," she was in the habit of saying. And Anjan agreed. She was younger, but far ahead of him as an artist. She'd had several solo shows in the best galleries. And his only solo was at the Academy of Fine Arts, where anyone could have an exhibition.

Anjan's thoughts went back to the phone call. Whoever it was, they'd called yesterday after he left—either just before or after Sundar received the news of his wife's sickness. In his haste to leave, he'd forgotten to close the window. And if by any chance it was Manna-da, why didn't he try calling today? Whatever the reason behind his attempt to reach him, it had to be an urgent one. *What could it be?* He hadn't seen the man since returning the book. And he hadn't been to his house in a long time. Who knew how the family was doing! He never found out why he'd resigned even though he was going to retire in just three years. Pijush didn't have a clue either. *How little he knew about the man!* And he didn't know his wife any better. In fact, he knew her even less, their interaction restricted by his role. Which, come to think of it, was of a sperm donor, wasn't it? *That* was who he was to them. *A seedpod!* And who wanted to reveal their true selves to a fucking seedpod?

A fucking seedpod! Anjan cringed at the thought, the images it led to. He remembered how matter-of-fact, almost businesslike, Renuka's behavior had been when they'd got to it. Once the set-up was in place, and all the lead-in small talk over beer (with him) and cups of tea (with her) was out of the way, it was a quick transaction of pleasure with a definite goal. It happened twice, a day apart. And she was in charge, both unhesitant and detached at the same time. Anjan had been the coy one, at least on the first day, unused as he was to being intimate to someone he wasn't close to. The last time he'd undressed in front of a woman was years ago. He'd done it in front of Brinda, his only girlfriend ever. And it wasn't *undressing*—it was ripping the clothes off each other's bodies before having the most amazing sex at least *he* had ever had. In all these years, he never understood how they—*she*—could've broken up almost immediately after that day.

"Your art looks like the work of someone who's sex-starved," Bhaskar told him once. He used a word Anjan had never heard before—*sublimation*. He'd written it down somewhere. "Get married or get a girlfriend, and your paintings will change," his wise friend had said. Anjan wasn't so sure, although he didn't argue, but he understood *sex-starved*. He *was* sex-starved! Why would he let himself be used by Manna-da and his wife if he wasn't? The book, and the whole story about *this nice woman I'd like you to meet some day*—he wasn't a fool! He was just...anyway. If Ranja had come into the picture a little earlier, he wouldn't have fallen into that rabbit hole. Just her presence in his work life, the way it was now, would've prevented that. Pijush thought as much. He knew the whole story—Anjan had told him; he couldn't have kept it from Pijush, of all people.

"You don't have to keep visiting them," he'd told Anjan when Bidisha was just two months old. "You don't have any obligation—you're not a family member!" Anjan had no illusions about that either. It was a strange sense of...*what was it?* decorum...that had made him stay in touch with the couple, and even visit them once when Renuka was pregnant. And he'd gone to the hospital the day Bidisha was born. "Your job is *done* as far as they're concerned," Pijush would say to him without hiding his irritation. "Do you want Bidisha to grow up knowing you as some kind of an *uncle* hanging off the edge of the family? A hard to explain appendage? Get out of their life and start your own. Talk to Ranja!"

She'd left. Which was quite a bit earlier than usual, but she'd finished all her tasks. And it wouldn't have been fair to let her either sit around in this stuffy place (although he would've loved it if she had), or do more than her share of the work. "Are you sure there's nothing else I can do?" she'd asked. "Yes, thank you," he'd said. Could she leave in that case? *Of course!*

Anjan put the sketchbook back in the drawer, checking it twice to make sure he'd locked it properly. He had this checking habit he tried to stop but couldn't. He started thinking about the place where the Mannas lived. The one-bedroom unit and its dimly-lit living room with three wicker chairs, a glass-top table, a divan, a plywood cabinet, and an old fridge. A calendar, framed pictures of Vladimir Lenin and Subhas Bose, and one of a dead family member, hung on the light-green walls, across which house lizards chased one another endlessly. As for the bedroom, which he'd seen twice, the only thing he remembered was how high the bed was.

It was Bidisha he was worried about. Never mind that she'd never know who he was. He'd made up his mind to do as Pijush said—he'd get out of their life. But he couldn't stop thinking about her. He'd held her in his arms just once. She was about five months old then—

really small and almost feather-light. He imagined her to be slightly bigger now, and hopefully heavier too. He wished he'd gone to their house at least once since Manna-da left SCL. He wanted to see her once again.

It was almost four by his watch. He knew that Pijush was at work, and so he dialed his number.

"Hi, it's me," he said as soon as Pijush picked up the phone. "Manna-da might have tried to reach me yesterday. And I'm thinking…what if it had something to do with Bidisha?"

"What makes you think so?" Pijush said.

"I don't know. I'm worried."

"Then go take a look."

"Go to their house?"

"Where else?"

"Okay!"

That was exactly what Anjan had wanted to do. Pijush's words gave him the courage he'd been lacking.

Within minutes, he was out of his office. The tightness in his stomach reminded him he hadn't eaten lunch—the potato curry and rice his mother packed for him. He'd taken the tiffin box out of his bag and put it on the sideboard, and then forgotten about it. The afternoon sun was unforgiving. The heat was going to spoil the food in no time. Anjan imagined the revolting smell it was going to give off when he'd open the box tomorrow.

He held his bag in front of his eyes to shade them from the glare of the sun as he walked to the bus stop. The tar on the road had melted unevenly. He felt his shoes sinking into it in some places. Sweat dribbled past his eyes, nose and mouth like rainwater, the shirt sticking to his body. He spotted a taxi near the bus stop and quickened his pace, but it was gone before he could get to it. A bus arrived a few minutes later. Not wanting to waste any more time waiting for a taxi, he got on board.

For the next forty minutes or so, his mind was like a matchstick caught in a rivulet of floodwater, random, unrelated thoughts swirling in his head. Bidisha's face, the unfinished swatches, Manna-da's voice (*Have you read this book? I'd like you to meet her!*), the buttons on Ranja's blouse, his drawings, Sundar's note, the open window (which had led him to believe Sundar had come to work; he'd forgotten to check if his bag was there). He thought about Renuka saying "He wanted a boy" (she'd said that when she was still in the hospital, and Manna-da wasn't around), *Have you had lunch yet?* The potato curry spoiling in the tiffin box. *He wanted a boy!*

Could he be harassing her because he hadn't got a son? Would he take proper care of Bidisha?

He got off the bus at the familiar stop. Within minutes, he was at the entrance to the old apartment building where the Mannas lived. The double-panel wooden door with its flaking green paint was ajar. Anjan pushed it open and eased himself in to the cool, dark hallway, which led to the six flights of stairs he had to climb. Narrowing his eyes for a better view, he groped his way to the bottom of the stairwell, taking care not to step on the old dog that slept there. The stairs were lit by daylight sifting through the grimy windowpanes on each landing. Anjan hoisted himself up the stairs as quickly as he could. At the foot of the last flight, he thought he caught a whiff of familiar smells—like those of the hair oil and talcum powder Renuka used. The smells thickened as he reached the top of the stairs, but they weren't quite as distinct anymore. They mingled with other, more pungent odors—flowers, incense sticks—like in a temple.

The flat in which the Mannas lived was the last one on the left. He walked toward its door at a slower pace, panting.

A lock hung on the door, shining in the light that came in through the open window at the far end of the corridor.

Anjan stood in front of the door, his mind blank for a moment or two. He took the lock in his hand and pulled at it. A moment later, he pulled at it again. Harder this time. He had no idea what to make of it. Had they left this place for good? There was no way he could find out. There was no way he could find out if Manna-da had been the caller. And if it was him, why had he tried to reach him? Was everything okay with them? Was everything okay with Bidisha? *Would he ever see her again?*

He walked over to the window. A startled pigeon flew out of the cornice as he leaned over the ledge. Below, the traffic of trams, buses, taxis, autorickshaws, motorbikes and pedestrians moved like debris in a half-clogged gutter, the noise billowing like dirty foam. Looking up, Anjan found the pigeon flying in nervous circles, its wings bright against the clear, blue sky.

He stood still, as if waiting for it to come back down.

THE COLOR OF NOON

The sunlight on the window ledge is the color of noon. The house is unusually quiet.

"Jane?" he calls softly, still lying in bed. No response. "Are you there?"

In the lane bellow, the tinkling of a rickshaw-wallah's bell comes closer. It stops near the door; the sound of rickshaw handles being lowered to the ground. *Is that her?* Jane works the night shift at a local nursing home. She comes home by nine every morning, and never goes out again until five thirty.

The footsteps stop in front of their door, then resume climbing. It's Mrs. Aratoon; she lives upstairs. Her old dog whimpers, barks weakly, then whimpers again.

It's twelve seventeen by the clock on his bedside table. Not yet time for Jane's afternoon nap. Not time for his mother to be back either. She teaches at a primary school in the neighborhood, and comes home after lunch. Two pigeons fly back to their perch outside the window and start fighting.

"Jane?" he calls more loudly. Still no response. *Thank God,* he thinks. He's glad no one is at home.

The head! It feels like a lump of sore clay. *It must be the booze.* Lying on his back, he presses it on both sides with the heel of his palms. He imagines kneading it like a potter kneads his clay, or the way Jane kneads her dough when she makes chapati. The throbbing stops for a moment, then returns as soon as he eases the pressure. Mrs. Aratoon's dog begins to whimper again. *She'll die one of these days, poor dog. Poor, sweet dog!* He doesn't remember her name anymore. He used to like playing with her when both of them were younger. He never wanted to have one himself. *Not after Lucky.* Losing her was terrible. It was like in that Harold Robbins story where the dog dies and the boy says he hates dogs because they die. Something like that. He hated losing Lucky.

The pigeons go on fighting. He imagines them using words. He imagines them screaming at each other using the nastiest of words he knows. His stock of cuss words surprises him. He wonders where he learned all these words, all these "unholy" words, as his mother calls them.

He gets up from bed and shuffles to the bathroom. Switching on the light, he stands in front of the mirror. His bladder hurts, but he cannot take his eyes off the face, the one staring at him through the dust-covered, spotted glass under the dim, yellow light.

"Winfred," it whispers. "Winfred…"

"Yes!" he says.

"You killed a man," the face says.

It was around eleven at night last night. They were on their way out of Ghalib Bar on Elliot Road. *Too many drinks, as always.* Ismail and Shibu had already got into the car, and Win was waiting for Munna to come out of the toilet. He heard a noise inside and knew something was wrong. But before he could get there, the toilet door burst open. It was Munna. He had a bag in his hand, which wasn't his. "Let's get out of here," he said and made for the door. "Quick!" Munna hissed. One of the waiters had gone into the toilet in the meantime; he came out and screamed, "Stop that man, he's killed someone!"

Munna was out of the bar, and Win was almost near the door when this fat man tumbled out of a booth. He stood blocking Win's path. "Hold it there," the man slurred, spreading out his arms like a kabaddi player. A big man with a soft, melon-like face. Win had to get him out of the way before the waiters could reach him. His whole body was shaking. He reached for the switchblade knife he always carried in his pocket. He wanted to take it out and hold it in front of him, so that the bugger wouldn't get close. But he did. He lunged forward, *the drunk bastard!* He threw himself at Win just as Win's hand was stretching out with the knife pointed toward him. He dropped the knife as soon as he felt it had touched the man's body—which part he couldn't tell. The man let out a strange noise and collapsed to the floor. Win leaped over his body and ran out.

Ismail had already started the car. Munna pushed open the rear door. "Get in," he shouted. "Fast!"

Within moments, they were on Rafi Ahmed Kidwai Road. Ismail made a sharp right turn just as the traffic lights changed to red.

Win was relieved he was sitting in Ismail's car instead of being pinned down by the waiters at Ghalib. Or beaten up. He cursed himself for touching the knife. *Why didn't he just push the bugger out of the way?* He was so unsteady a single push would have done the job. *But, no, he had to take out the fucking knife!* "This knife will get you into trouble one day," Jane had told him many times. Why didn't he listen to her and stop carrying the damn thing? He remembered the man he'd bought it from; he remembered that shriveled-raisin face of his. Another one of those Sudder Street tourists. He said he was a retired sailor from Australia. "I have no use for this beauty anymore," he'd said about the knife. "I need some cash for my trip to the hills." Win remembered that scratchy voice of his. It sounded like the man had gargled with pieces of glass, and some were still stuck in his throat. He remembered the look on his face as he was counting the money Win had just given him. He'd borrowed it from Jane, promising to return it soon, which he never did. *What a mistake the whole thing was!*

Ismail was driving like crazy. His father's old Padmini whined and sputtered trying to run as fast as it could. He's the only one in the gang who even knows how to drive—he's from that type of family. The type that owns cars, shops, tanneries, and who knows what else. The rest of them cannot even dream about such things.

Inside the car, silence. Win had no idea where they were going. "Where are we going?" he finally asked.

"To fucking hell!" Ismail barked. "I keep telling you guys not to drink so much and get into bawals!"

"It had nothing to do with drinking." Munna tried to sound calm. "I just hit the bugger in the face. It knocked him out, but he'll be okay. If you knew how he screwed my life you'd be surprised I didn't break his neck today."

"*Screwed your life!*" Ismail hissed. "Now wait and see how *this* screws your life. And ours too! Who knows if there wasn't an off-duty *mamu* sitting there and watching your drama? We can all end up in Lal Bazar because of you! And you stole the guy's bag?"

"At least that!" Munna said.

"And Win?" Ismail tilted his head at the window.

Win was directly behind him, trapped in the smell of tanned leather that always hangs around him. Everything that belongs to Ismail carries that smell; it goes wherever he goes. The smell reminded Win of Ismail's house, the godown full of leather, rolls and rolls of it everywhere.

"This fat bugger sitting near the door got in the way," he said.

"And?"

"I think I...nicked him." Win couldn't believe he said that.

"The chap with curly hair and glasses? Alone, right?"

"Yeah. In a black T-shirt."

"Fuck!" Ismail screamed. "I think I *know* the man!"

They reached the Eden Gardens. Ismail slowed the car. No one spoke. They sat still, looking over their shoulders from time to time to see if they were being followed. The street was flooded with neon light. The Maidan club tents, the rickety wooden galleries and the stadium on the other side loomed in the still night like monsters about to wake from their sleep.

They circled the area, drove up and down Strand Road and crossed the Howrah Bridge several times. After about an hour, Ismail stopped the car in front of a godown in Bara Bazar. He'd spotted a little space between two big trucks loaded with goods. He parked the car there, and turned off the engine. It stopped with a tired, raspy sigh. The two gigantic vehicles hid the car from streetlight, which made Win feel safer than when they were driving.

Ismail lit a cigarette and took a long drag. "He looked familiar," he said. "But not sure why. Maybe I've seen him with Baba. Maybe one of his customers." He took a few more drags, then passed the cigarette to Shibu. It was obvious who he was talking about—not Munna's man, but Win's.

A fresh wave of anxiety crashed on Win's chest. The jolt made his heart start to race again. He started to think, once again, about how easily he could have got out of that place without hurting the man. All he needed to do was just push the guy out of the way. Just one big shove, and he would've been back down in his booth. Win would've been inside the car by the time he could get himself on his feet again. The man was too drunk to be any real threat, but he was too scared to see it at the time. *Too fucking scared!* He clenched his jaw. A cold sweat trickled down his body where the shirt didn't touch his skin.

It was past one in the morning when Win got out of the car on S.N. Banerjee Road. He wanted to walk, he told Ismail.

Smith Lane was quiet. The area close to their house was darker than usual; at least one streetlight wasn't working. And no one seemed to be awake except Bahadur, the Nepali night watchman. "Hello, Vinshab, everything okay?" he called out the way he always does, as if there's always a chance something is not okay. *But didn't he sound slightly different? Like there was a reason why he was asking him if everything was alright?* Win raised his hand in reply and quickly slipped into the passage leading to the main door. He unlocked the door, stepped in and pushed the door gently shut. The stairwell was pitch-dark, but he didn't switch on the lights. He was used to coming home late and feeling his way up four flights of wooden stairs to get to their flat.

He stood in front of the door for a few moments, the smaller of the two keys held between his thumb and forefinger. He eased it into the lock and turned it as softly as he could. He pushed the door just enough to let himself in quietly. Inside, the darkness was alive with the sound of his mother's snores. He filled his lungs with the warm, soothing scent of home—the air heavy with the smell of food, talcum powder and soap. The nightmare at Ghalib seemed distant and unreal, as if it *was* a real nightmare, and he'd just woken up from it.

He took off the shoes and tiptoed into his room. As he lay down on the bed, he felt himself sinking into a darkness that spun like a whirlpool.

"You killed a man," the face in the mirror says again.

No, wait! It was probably just a nick on his chest. Maybe a small gash. It couldn't kill a big man like him. No way! I didn't push the knife. Maybe they took him where Jane works. Maybe that's why...she isn't home yet? God!

Somebody is at the door. He's sure he heard a knock—a light one, the way Shibu does it. Everyone in the gang has a different way of knocking the door, and Shibu does it only once and so lightly you can miss it sometimes. But Win is sure he heard it.

"Come in," he says to Shibu, opening the door, then runs back to the bathroom to pee.

"Hurry up," Shibu says.

"Okay, tell me," Win says, flushing the toilet and washing his hands. "What happened?"

"We're fucked."

Shibu takes out a folded sheet of newspaper from his pocket and hands it to Win. "Take a look."

Win spreads the paper on the table, smoothing it hurriedly with both palms. "Where is it?"

"At the bottom. Left side. That one there. He's in the ICU. The police are looking for us."

"It says local medical center," Win says, reading across a patch where the paper has soaked up the dampness from his fingers. "Doesn't say exactly where. I have a feeling they took him where my sister works. That's the only hospital in that area. Listen, I'm going to get out of here now."

"Where are you going?"

"No idea. Maybe to a friend's place in Howrah. And stay there for a few days. I don't know."

Win is surprised he said Howrah. The friend who lives there is Gopi Nath Rai, someone he hasn't seen in a long time—at least two or three years. They used to be close in school, then life took them in different directions. The last time they met, Gopi talked about his job in the railways, and his wedding, which was around the corner. "You have to come," Gopi had said. He'd sent an invitation too, but Win didn't go. He sent a card with an apology and a false excuse. He doesn't remember what he'd said about why he couldn't come, but the real reason was, he didn't want to embarrass himself. They belonged in different places in life—Gopi had made it, and he...well, he did the exact opposite of what his name means. His pet name, that is, the shorter version of his real name. *He hates it!* Every time he hears someone say it (except his mother and Jane, and his friends), it sounds like they're making fun of him. Like, hidden under the sound of Win is its opposite meaning. Like, if they could, they'd call him Lose instead—*Hey, Lose!* Or even better, *Loser!* Showing up at Gopi's wedding would've made that obvious, the difference between the two of them, their places in life. And the ridiculous falseness of his name.

Shibu has left. Of course, he wouldn't go to Gopi's! *And stay there for a few days?* What was he thinking?

The pigeons are at it again. He can hear them just as clearly from near the table, which is in front of the kitchen, between the bathroom and the two bedrooms. A narrow table covered with a sheet of rose printed plastic and three chairs. This is where they eat, watched by his black & white father and colored Jesus. Win stands there for a few more minutes, trying to think through things. Things he needs to do now—decide where he's going to go, and for how long.

The sound of footsteps on the stairs makes his thoughts stop. He rushes back into his room and waits near the door, a hand on the door knob. *What if it's Jane?* What if it's his mother? *Or the police?* Should he close the door? He can hear his heart thumping.

As the footsteps come closer, they sound like Mr. Aratoon's. The sound of both feet landing on the same step, two thuds close to each other. But the man has been dead for years. Maybe a brother of his? *But he didn't have a brother!* Maybe a relative then? Or a friend? Or a *fucking* ghost? He's heard his mother talk about hearing ghostly footsteps in the house. Who knows! Win is glad it's not either her or Jane, or anyone looking for him. He closes the door and pulls out his kitbag from the top of his almirah. He gives it a shake to get rid of the dust, then quickly fills it with a pair of jeans, two shirts, underwear, and socks, all of them unwashed, giving off a musty smell. He realizes he didn't change out of his clothes last night, so he's ready. *Ready to run away from home.*

A shiver runs down his spine. He's never had to even *think* of doing such a thing before. His hands and legs begin to feel unsure, as if he's about to lose control over them. He's been in trouble before, but nothing ever as serious as this. He sneezes—once, twice, three times, four times. It's the dust from the bag.

On his way out, he slips into the bedroom his mother shares with Jane. Both windows in the room are closed, the smell of Ponds in the stale air, the talcum powder his mother uses. Switching on the light, he walks to Jane's bed and lifts the mattress. She keeps all her money there in a plastic bag. He takes out a hundred-rupee note and a few ten-rupee ones and drops the mattress. Then lifts it again to put two ten-rupee notes back in the bag. He's left with three more, plus the hundred, which is enough. It's all *her* money after all—he shouldn't have touched it in the first place. But he did, as he always does, and never returns any of it. Like the amount he'd borrowed to buy that *fucking knife*. He'd *borrowed* it, promising he was going to give it back, but didn't. He steps out of the flat with a stab of guilt, and pulls the door shut.

"Where are you going?" Jane says, panting. She's on the landing below, her left hand gripping the banister.

The last thing Win wanted was to run into his sister now. "To Gopi's house," he says hastily.

"Gopi?" Jane frowns.

"Gopi Nath, you know, my—"

"How come? You haven't seen him in years!"

"I saw him yesterday."

"Why are you taking the bag?"

"He said, bring a change of clothes. I want you to meet a friend, he said. A businessman, who's looking for people. He said, maybe—"

"When will you be back?"

"Tomorrow." He climbs down the stairs, relieved he didn't have to cook up more lies to more questions.

"Bye," he says, walking past her.

"Bye," Jane says and begins to trudge up the stairs.

She looks weak and old, almost like their mother. Win feels sad. *Poor Jane!* She's been working like a dog ever since their father died. Couldn't finish college, and took a nursing job so that there was food on the table and money for her brother's school. That was twelve years ago. Now she's thirty-four—*only nine years older than him*—but climbs stairs like someone twice her age. Who knows how long she'll last if things go on like this! Why didn't he think about all this before? Why didn't he...? *Too late, too late now!*

"Jane?" he calls from the landing below. He wants to ask why she was so late today. Was she held up at work for some emergency? Did something come up last night? "Where's Mum?"

"Gone to see Reverend Simon," she says, unlocking the door. "Should be back in an hour."

"Okay, and...um...I took some dough." He leans on the banister, craning his neck. "Hundred thirty."

"Okay."

"Thanks." Win runs down the stairs.

Shibu said Ismail had sent him with that newspaper page. He didn't have to tell Win that; it was obvious. Shibu couldn't have found that report himself. He doesn't read newspapers. And in English? *No way!* He and Munna—they'd never pick up a paper even out of curiosity, unless there's a picture of a Bollywood goddess there. They just listen to the radio, those two. Always glued to their pocket-sized transistor sets, listening to film songs. With him, it's a different story. In his family, reading The Statesman is like going to church. You *cannot* not do it. Win is the only one who doesn't. He doesn't read the paper and he doesn't go to church. He thinks it makes him a bit like Ismail, who smells of leather all the time but doesn't eat meat. Not even chicken. *Crazy!* But Win thinks it's also special—it's one of the many things he likes about the man. Coming from his background, he shouldn't be hanging around with them. But he does. Not only that, he's extremely protective of them, almost like a big brother. Who pays for all the grub and booze when they go somewhere? *Ismail, of course.* He just doesn't like it when they get drunk and things happen. Like last night.

He gets off the tram in Dharmatala. The afternoon sun is beating down on the chaos and noise of trams, buses, taxis, cars and pedestrians. The smell of street food reminds him of his empty stomach. He hasn't had a morsel since Ghalib. He hears the conductor of a minibus screaming *Howrah, Howrah, Howrah, Howrah* and begins to push his way through the crowd to get to the bus. It starts to move, and he breaks into a run. Picking up speed, he catches up to it and grabs hold of the handlebar, while still running. The conductor makes room for him on the footboard and helps him up. He's boarded running buses like this all his life, but doesn't like doing it. He's seen things happen in front of him— people losing their grip on the handlebar and slipping off the footboard, getting close to being run over. Every time he gets on a bus like this, he fears the same thing happening to him.

The bus is not crowded, although most of the seats are occupied. He finds one at the back and slumps down on it, his heart thumping.

"Ticket?" the conductor holds out his hand.

"Howrah station." Win hands him a ten-rupee note, wondering why he said that. *Why did he even board this bus?* He's not going to Gopi's house! He wonders if his mother is back home yet. He imagines the two of them talking—his mother and Jane:

Where's Win?

He's gone to Gopi Nath's house.

Who?

Gopi Nath Rai, Mum. His friend from St James'. Remember?

No, I don't.

Said Gopi invited him to meet a friend for a job or something.

A lie!

How's Father Simon?

Please tell your darling brother to get a real job or get out of this house. Okay? Enough is enough!

I will, Mum. Tell me about Father now. Is he alright?

A bit better. But you know how these people are, Maria and her husband. They just don't know how to nurse people properly. Low-caste Anglos! Not educated enough, that's the problem.

Win can feel the corners of his mouth stretching into a thin smile. The bus is stuck in a traffic jam in Bara Bazar. Looking out of the window he recognizes the place where they'd parked between the trucks last night. He remembers the sense of relief he'd felt when Ismail squeezed the car into that dark spot and turned off the engine. How *safe* it felt to be there for a few moments, hidden from light! Now the place is filled with harsh sunlight, street vendors and noise.

He told Shibu to tell Ismail he'd try to call tonight.

"If I can't do it tonight, tell him I'll do it tomorrow," he said. "Tell him I won't be at home. I'll be in Howrah."

Howrah! That's where he's headed now, but he has no idea why. He thinks of the knife. *I have no use for this beauty anymore.* He remembers the man's name—*Kevin Hogg.* Who knows what's happened to the knife. Maybe the police took it for investigation. Or maybe in all that confusion, people forgot about it and it's still lying there on the floor. In a dark corner, where the sweeper's broom doesn't reach, a rat or two licking at the dried blood on the blade. And who knows where Kevin Hogg is! Did he ever use Win's money—*Jane's* money—to go to the hills?

Boats. He can see several of them. Small fishing boats with open cabins and tarpaulin-covered roofs. The bus is almost near the middle of the bridge, and is hardly moving because of another jam. The woman next to him had the window seat—she left before the bus got on the bridge. Win is glad she did. He loves the way the river looks. He could sit there just like that and keep looking at the water, and its changing colors—muddy gold, green, gray, silver. There's a bit of cloud in the sky, a warm haze hanging in the air. The breeze on his face feels damp. He stares at the bright blue roof of a tiny boat as it edges closer to the bank. Below him, a bigger one makes its way from under the bridge down the middle of the river. A passenger boat.

A passenger boat! He was once on a boat like that, going in the same direction—a long time ago, almost thirteen years. They were going to the botanical gardens. The Aratoons were also there. It was a January day, just after their Christmas—the 5th or the 6th of January, Win doesn't remember exactly when. Christmas in January is a strange idea anyway, but that's when the Aratoons celebrated it, and invited his family every year. His father loved drinking rum with Mr. Aratoon, who worked at the Armenian College. He said he was from Iran, and had come to Calcutta as a small boy. He said he'd been to many places in the world, but loved Calcutta the most. This is where I want to die, he said. And he did.

Why is he thinking about it now? He wonders if it's because of the footsteps he heard in the morning. Father Simon was also with them on the boat, and a few other people. His father never liked the man much, Father Simon. Jane said it was because he thought Father flirted with Mum. "Not true, of course," she said. Win had no clue. He just didn't like the funny way Father pronounced his mother's name, as if it was a Bengali name— *Maargareet!*

By next Christmas, their father was gone. The day was 11th November, 1983. And life changed forever.

The bus has started to move again. He can still make out that passenger boat in the crowd of boats in the distance. A thicker crowd of pedestrians at the end of the bridge. He'd have to do it someday, he thinks, cross the bridge on foot and see how it feels. Maybe stand in the middle for some time and look down. The thought sends a shiver down his spine. Suddenly, a rat's twitching nose and whiskers, and its hungry eyes, fill his field of vision— like a closeup on a movie screen, larger than life, gigantic, stretching across everything he can see. The eyes, the twitching nose and whiskers, and crusted blood.

The bus is nearing its stop. Everyone has stood up; Win also gets up from his seat. He tries to get rid of the image, but cannot. The noise that came out of the man's mouth when he collapsed to the floor—Win can hear it through all the honking of the buses, trucks, and taxis.

How is he now? He was in the ICU—what if he never comes out? *What if he has children at home?*

Win finds himself in the middle of a crowd rushing toward the entrance to the station. He doesn't have a train to catch, but he walks hurriedly to keep himself from getting in the way of people. Although he doesn't have a destination, he feels like he's one of them. He feels like he's part of the crowd—like a cell in a body, like a drop in a river—part of it in a way that makes him completely unknown. And hidden.

A nudge on his shoulder wakes Win. A face with a long, white beard and a big yellow turban with things written on it. A sadhu. The same one he'd sat down next to on the steps going up to the ticket counters.

He'd called Ismail's number twice from the phone booth inside, and both times it was his father, so Win had hung up without saying a word. And he wanted to talk to Jane—he wanted to ask her about the man, but it was still too early for her to be at work, so he had no choice but to wait. Back outside, he'd found a bit of space on the steps at the entrance. The sadhu was sitting there with a cloth sack, a plastic bag and a walking stick. He pulled those things closer to himself and made more room for Win, inviting him to sit down. A family was sitting on the other side. He remembered thanking the man, and feeling glad there was a pillar behind him to rest his back against.

He has no idea how long he slept, but the sun has set. The family has left; there are other people sitting there now. The sadhu is still there, his face right in front of Win's. He's smiling, his right hand holding a paper plate full of puris and curry, steam rising from them. The smell makes Win feel like...if he doesn't take the plate himself within a moment or two, his stomach was going to grow an arm of its own and send it up through his chest and throat, and shoot it out of his mouth to snatch it from the sadhu's hand.

"Thank you," Win says weakly, taking the plate. "Shukriya!" He keeps holding it in front of him, staring at the man's face in disbelief.

The sadhu smiles and motions him to start eating.

MOVIE STAR

They said he was a movie star. And every time you saw him, you thought, *Of course!* How could he *not* be one? That height, those looks! He was six foot something, taller than everyone around him, and had the most handsome, perfectly chiseled face anyone had ever seen. Plus the clothes he wore—always stylish and well-fitting, and freshly ironed, as if he never wore anything twice before sending it to the dhobi. And the way he carried himself, the way he walked, and talked to people. The voice he had, and the smile. The way he *smelled*—it was so good, you wanted to stick to his side, or walk behind him as long as you could.

He had to have been in the movies!

But did anyone ever see films in which he'd acted? Could anyone name a picture? That no one could, didn't matter. Not to *us,* anyway. We were—how old were we then? Eleven, twelve? I was eleven, give or take a few months, and so were Andy and Mush (short for Mushtaq). Raju and Bapi were slightly older, twelve or thirteen, and Rustam and Bob were younger. To us, these seven kids—two Anglo-Indian (Andy and I), one Bihari (Mush), two Bengali (Raju and Bapi), one Parsi (Rustam) and one Chinese (Bob)—Sikandar Khan was...forget movie star, he was bigger. He was God! And we *worshipped* the man. He was different from everyone we knew, whether in the neighborhood or anywhere else. There was nothing about him that was ordinary, including his name. He was no one's uncle, or chacha, or bhaia, or anything of that sort. He was simply Sikandar Khan. You called him either Mr. Khan or Khan-sahb, depending on who you were. Bob's father, John Chung, who owned a shoe shop on Bentinck Street, called him Mr. Sikandar Khan—*Hello, Mr. Sikandar Khan*, he'd go.

This was '75 or '76. And it wasn't as if Sikandar Khan had just moved to our neighborhood. His family had been living there forever. Khan Furniture, which his father owned, was one of Janbazar's oldest establishments. The family lived in a big old house on the corner where Temple Street met Chandni Chowk Street. And everybody knew them. Especially his father, who'd been one of the most prosperous businessmen in the area. I used to hear my dad and his friends, most of whom either owned small businesses or worked in them, mention the Khans in their conversations, although I never cared about exactly what they said. I wasn't interested in their gossip. Until one day I heard Dad say to Mum, "Really sad what poor Mr. Khan (*Sikandar Khan's father*) is going through. First his wife and now a son!" His voice was different. It didn't have the usual tightness of envy when he talked about the Khans. Apparently, the man had just lost his older son. His wife had died less than a year ago.

None of my friends knew any of this. Except Mush, who also knew that the dead man's younger brother, Sikandar Khan, who spent a lot of time in Bombay, would permanently move back to Calcutta. "Shut up!" Andy would bark. "Don't pretend you know people you don't." Mush would stutter and stammer in protest, but would get shouted down by Andy and the rest of the gang, myself included.

Then I saw him one day. *Sikandar Khan!* He was walking down Madan Street. I was on my way back from school. I recognized him right away because I'd seen him before—not too many times, but often enough to know who he was. Although that was the first time I *really* noticed him. Because of all the stuff I'd heard about him and his family just a month or so ago. And Mush had mentioned him a few times since then, saying he was coming back from Bombay. "Hey, Mushy-Mush was right, man," I said to Andy when I saw him that afternoon on Shaheed Minar Ground. It was a Saturday. Andy, Raju and I had gone there to play cricket with a bunch of other kids. "Sikandar Khan is back from Bombay!" I said. Raju said he'd seen him too. Later, we found out that Mush knew everything because his father, who had a tailoring shop on Bertram Street, knew the Khans. They'd been his clients for years.

That was how our fascination with the man had started, replacing all our old obsessions—cricket, kites, fish tanks. And it also made us more interested in the movies. People said Sikander Khan had a great future in Bombay. And that, if he wasn't forced to come back, because there was no one to look after his father and his business, he'd have gone far. We believed that without bothering to find out if it was true. We never asked questions. After all, didn't he look just as good as Vinod Khanna? Or Shatrughan Sinha? "Far better, man," Andy would say. "Look at him and look at them. Heaven and hell, man! They can't hold a candle to him."

None of us disagreed. We were star-struck. And what helped us stay that way was that, almost every day, at least one of us would spot him somewhere. Now that he was back for good, you ran into him all the time. The other thing that helped was gossip. The things people said about him, good or bad. Before Sikandar Khan came into the picture, I'd never paid attention to what the grown-ups talked about. My friends hadn't either. But now we were hungry for stories. We pricked up our ears whenever there was a hint of gossip.

And it was everywhere. In that strange world of shops and homes, where businesses and families flowed into one another like muddy streams in the monsoon, everyone knew everyone else. Including the fruit sellers, who sat on the footpath, and the men who sold syrupy, red and green soft drinks on that bustling stretch of Madan Street. Gossip hummed like flies on the piles of mango and papaya. If you were in the right place at the right time, you heard all kinds of juicy details about people who lived and worked in the area—what they were up to, who was fleecing their customers, who was going around with whom, and so on. As for us, we had no interest in stories about other people. They all went in one ear and out the other. But the moment we heard anyone mention the name Sikandar Khan—or Khan-sahb, or just Khan—our inner tape recorders got switched on. *Like that!* It was automatic. We didn't have to do anything ourselves. His name always pressed the right button in our heads.

Soon, each one of us had their own bag of Sikandar Khan stories. Some of which were similar, some not. Sometimes, each one had a different version of the same story. Like the one about the man's affair with Salma. The widowed daughter of Mansoor Khairullah, another big businessman in our area. In Andy's story, she'd eloped with Sikandar Khan, and had a child who was being raised by a distant aunt of hers somewhere in Gujarat. In Mush's version, they were only good friends, because their families had known one another for years. Mine and Bapi's were the most exciting of the lot. They were also quite similar, although we'd picked them up from different sources. I'd heard (from the son of one my father's friends) that Salma had gone missing for months after her husband's death. He'd died in a car accident. This was sometime in the late 60s, when we were too young to know any of this. Sikandar Khan had already been living in Bombay. He'd arranged for Salma to go there on her own so that they could get married. Apparently, their families were against their wish to be together. Bapi said, "He'd come to Calcutta secretly to take her to Bombay by car." I never found out where he'd heard the story, but it matched some of the details of mine: Salma had fled to Bombay to be with Sikandar Khan. But they never got married, and never had a child.

Even if only a small part of the story was true (although we believed *a lot of it* was), it was a huge thing. The Khairullahs were not just wealthy, they were also an educated lot. Salma, the only sister of four brothers, had graduated from Loreto College. And she was the prettiest woman anyone had seen in that part of town. Although *I* thought Christine Rogers was equally pretty. She taught at Loreto Dharamtala, and lived not far from where the Khans did on Temple Street. But anyway, Salma Khairullah was drop-dead gorgeous. "She's as sharp as she's pretty," I'd heard Mum say about her once. All of that just made Sikandar Khan look larger than life to us. Who else could do such a thing in real life? *It happened only in the movies!*

But there were things we'd found out about him that we *knew* were true. Things about how kind and generous he was. Bob said Sikandar Khan bought all his shoes from his father's shop, and paid for each pair even though his father hadn't returned the money he'd borrowed from the man years ago. "Last year he gave my dad more money because business wasn't good," Bob said. We knew—again, thanks to Bob himself—that Mr. Chung hadn't managed to pay Sikandar Khan back.

Meanwhile, our curiosity about the movies he might have acted in kept growing. Every now and then, someone would say they'd seen him in a new film. And that would make us go completely mad with excitement. We'd go see the film as soon as we could. Rustom and Bob couldn't always come with us because they were younger, but the rest of us would no matter what. We'd cut school and sneak into a noon show at Elite, or Paradise, or wherever else it happened to be playing. Only to come back disappointed, and angry at whoever had spread the lie. But we never learned our lesson. Every time we heard a rumor like that, we thought, *Maybe this time it's true! If it isn't, we won't listen to such rubbish again.*

The strangest thing of all was that we never managed to ask the man himself if he'd really acted in a film. Andy, the bravest among us, had tried to do it a couple of times, but backed down at the last minute. The aura of the man was too hypnotic—you just stood there staring at him, and got tongue-tied if you tried to speak. Even though he was right there in our midst, it seemed as if we were separated by an invisible distance, which we didn't have the courage to cross.

Life went on. Things happened around us, both good and bad. Raju, who went to St. Mary's, made it to his school's cricket team in '78. He was an allrounder, but his bowling—man, the boy was quick!—was better than his batting. Thanks to his performance, St. Mary's, which never had a good team, went quite far in the summer school cricket tournament two years in a row—'78 and '79. And in both seasons, Raju's name appeared in the papers. *Unbelievable!* One of *our* names in the papers? Who would have thought it was possible? The first year he took 7 wickets in a match, which included a hattrick— three wickets in three consecutive balls! The next year, he did great with the bat too, and got written about twice. Andy was sure Raju would've made it to the Bengal under-16 team if he weren't a bit older. "But you wait and see," he said, "he'll play for Bengal in a few years." I was also convinced that he would.

The same year—'79—Bapi lost his mother. Strangely, we didn't know that she'd been sick for a while. We used to go to his house a lot when we were younger. The attraction was this huge fish tank they had next to the tube well behind their kitchen. It was full of all kinds of plants and fish. We'd crouch down on the ground, put our chins on the tank's low cement wall and get lost in that magical world. For whatever reason, he never took us to his room or to any other room in their house. He'd let us into the building through a side door, and lead us down a narrow passage past the kitchen and into the tiny backyard. The death of his mother changed him. He wasn't the boy he used to be.

Around the same time, we started to hear that Bob's family might leave for Hong Kong. "Dad is tired of borrowing money to run the shop," Bob said. "The Puja sales were terrible this year." The months before Durga Puja were when the shoe shops on Bentinck Street were the busiest. All shop owners counted on business around that time. "No one buys Chinese shoes anymore," he said. "Everyone wants Bata. Dad is saying we should go."

One afternoon, Bob was waiting for us in his father's shop. Raju, Andy, Rustom and I were on our way there. The plan was to go to the Maidan after that. Rustam was talking about his uncle's friend who worked in a production house in Bombay. And thanks to this friend, he—*his uncle*—had met a few stars. "Zeenat Aman, Shashi Kapoor, Helen, Dharmendra," he said. "They even invited him to their parties—not my uncle, of course, but his friend." So Rustam was saying that this friend of his uncle's, whatever his name was, *knew* Sikander Khan. "'Sikandar Khan from Calcutta, right?' my uncle's friend said, 'Of course, I know him' he said. 'My God,' he said, 'he had so many affairs here with all these stars!'" The story was that one of these stars (Rustam couldn't remember who) would've married him if he hadn't left Bombay all of a sudden. "All rubbish!" Andy said. "I don't believe any of this." "Maybe it's true, who knows?" I said. "Of course, it's true," Rustom said.

We were in the middle of this, and were about to turn right on Madan Street, when we heard some hullaballoo on the other side. "Look, Sikander Khan!" Raju said. There was a crowd in front of Ram Laha's crockery store. Sikander Khan stood out because he was a foot and a half taller than everyone around him. We ran across the street, dodging taxis and motorbikes. A man lay on the footpath, groaning and bleeding from the nose. Ram Laha's son (we never found out what his name was) was screaming at the top of his lungs. "How dare you do this inside my shop?" he said to the man. "Calm down," Sikander Khan said to him, grabbing his arm and guiding him back into his shop. "How much did he take" he asked. It was a hot day. Sikander Khan's forehead was beaded with sweat, his white kameez stuck to his body. "One hundred and twenty-five rupees, sahb," one of his employees said. "It was *my* money," he said. "Did you get it back?" Sikander Khan asked. The man said he'd searched the thief's pockets and found the money. "Next time I see you around here, I'll break your legs!" Ram Laha's son screamed out of his shop. "Khamosh!" Sikander Khan said, raising his voice. "Enough! Get back to your work now." No one had ever heard him sound angry. Everyone shut up. Including the thief. "Where are you from?" he asked the thief. The man mumbled something, which Sikander Khan didn't understand. He looked around and motioned to a rickshaw-wallah he knew. He asked him to take the thief to his house so that his servant could give him something to eat. He said he would be home shortly.

The whole thing couldn't have lasted more than ten minutes. But we kept talking about it for days and weeks after that. What blew our minds was not how he'd stopped the quarrel, which wasn't difficult for him anyway. But the fact that he'd sent the thief to his own house. *Knowing* that he'd stolen money, and had been caught red-handed. *Who would ever do such a thing?*

We found out later that he'd given the man a job in Khan Furniture.

***

"Mr. Khan passed away," Mum said as soon as I walked in.

It was a Sunday. I'd just come back from the Maidan. Raju and I had gone there to watch some kite-flying. We'd stopped flying kites ourselves, but liked watching others do that now and then. "What are you talking about?" I almost screamed at Mum. She explained that it was Sikander Khan's father. He'd been sick and was in a hospital. "They've just brought the body home," Mum said. "Dad's gone there to pay his last respects."

What we couldn't have guessed at the time was that this would be the beginning of a new chapter in the Sikander Khan story. Suddenly, he wasn't that visible anymore. And if you ran into him somewhere by chance, he avoided eye contact. He looked more distant than before, and rarely stopped for a chat. Mush said his father thought Sikander Khan was suffering from some disease. "Man, he looks so thin, doesn't he?" Andy said one day when we spotted him getting on a rickshaw. We all agreed. And we suddenly realized that, whenever we saw him now, we saw him on a rickshaw. Also, people weren't talking about his acting career anymore. New pictures came from Bombay without any rumor of Sikander Khan being in them.

What people talked about now was what was happening to Khan Furniture. Instead of running it himself after his father's death, Sikander Khan had put one of their old employees in charge. His name was Rashid, who had been a favorite of Sikander Khan's father. But the man was too old to manage the business, so before long it was his son, Aftab, who was running the show. And the thief, whom Sikander Khan had rescued from Ram Laha's shop, did all the physical work. He was from a village in the south. "A good man," Mush told us. "If it wasn't for him, Khan Furniture would be empty by now." What he'd found out was that Aftab was selling stuff off behind Sikander Khan's back, and pocketing the cash. And this man (his name was Kanu) would count every piece of furniture when the shop opened and closed every day. There was a constant battle between him and Aftab. "Kanu is repaying his debt to Khan-sahb," Mush said. "He's doing his best to protect his boss's interests."

Soon, it became clear to many in the area that poor Kanu was fighting a losing battle. One day, Dad got so worked up he went to see Sikandar Khan in his house. Apparently, the man listened to my father patiently and thanked him for his concern, saying that he *knew* everything but couldn't say anything to Aftab. "Rashid is not well," he said to my dad. "And I don't have the money to help him." So, allowing Aftab to do what he was doing was the only way he could offer help. "They need the money more than I do," he'd said. "But Kanu doesn't understand. He always fights with Aftab." He asked Dad not to worry. "The inventory is large enough to survive this crisis. Aftab won't be able to sell the whole shop."

The man's image changed in our eyes. He was no more the hero-like figure he'd been. The luster had gone. He looked old and weak.

We, too, had changed. For one thing, we'd suddenly become embarrassingly hairy. All of us, except Bob. Even Rustam, who was younger, had a thin moustache now. Raju had started to shave. The first time he'd done it he looked like a shaved cat. Our reaction made him laugh, which made him look worse. The fear of looking like that kept me away from the razor for a long time. Besides, I had a thin face, and the downy fuzz that covered it now made it look a bit fuller. So I didn't mind it. But I'd stopped wearing shorts, except when I was playing football. Apart from hair growth, there were other things happening in our worlds, which pulled us in different directions. The focus of each one of us had shifted from Sikander Khan to whatever was new in our lives.

In mine it was Shibani Banerjee. A Class XI student of Loreto Dharamtala, and a favorite of Ms. Rogers, who'd become the school's new principal. She'd said yes to me; I couldn't believe my luck. We went to the movies. Globe, Light House, the New Empire, wherever they played Hollywood films—Shibani hated Hindi cinema. We ate papdi chaat, and listened to the Bee Gees and Nazia Hassan. She was crazy about disco. A Bengali Brahmin, she went to church with us. She knew the Lord's Prayer by heart, and sang all the hymns without looking at the text. Mum started saying, "She's not an Anglo, but I wouldn't mind having her as my daughter-in-law." "Too early, Linda, too early," Dad would say.

I'm grateful to God for this, I'd say to myself. *I don't want anything more out of life!* I couldn't imagine being happier than I was. I was my parents' only child; we were a solid trio. And now there was Shibani.

Before I knew it, almost two years had passed. I finished my first year of B.Com. at St. Xavier's, and she ranked 7th in her ISC exams. She'd been talking about applying to both Presidency and St. Xavier's. She wanted to study mathematics. "Please come to St. Xavier's," I'd plead. Although with those results, she could now get into any college she wanted. And Presidency might in fact be better for her. "My uncle teaches math in the US," she said to me one day. "He wants me to go to his university."

This was toward the end of May, a week or so after her results had come out. We were walking around the Victoria Memorial gardens. The sun was about to set, but it was still very hot. I was sweating badly. My heart skipped a beat when I heard that. *A university in the US, my God!* That would be so good for her. She was a star student, and deserved the best higher education she could get. *But on the other hand....* I couldn't think anymore. I wanted to change the subject, talk about something else. "Andy's band is playing at a classmate's birthday party tomorrow," I remember saying. "If you have time, we could go there."

We'd spent the rest of our time that evening talking about Andy and his band.

Meanwhile, Rustom and his family had left Calcutta. This had come as a big surprise because unlike Bob he never talked about leaving. His family, unlike the Chungs, didn't have any problems, at least not any we knew about. So we weren't prepared for the news, which made it doubly sad. And I was sure that if it had happened a couple of years earlier, when we were younger and closer, before Shibani had come into my life, it would have been devastating. Raju and I talked about how quickly our life had changed. I missed Rustam.

Shibani got busy preparing for her GRE and TOEFL. Whenever we met—which, all of a sudden, was not that often anymore, because she was busy—she talked about all the stuff she was hearing from her uncle. America, university life, how hard she'd have to work if she got admission. And of course, financial aid—she said she couldn't go unless she got a full scholarship. Secretly, I started to hope she wouldn't get one. *Please, please, God,* I prayed. I also felt guilty and miserable for doing that, and begged for forgiveness. Mum caught on to what was going on, and asked me what the problem was. I told her everything, which made her cry.

One day in early January, 1985, I stood on the visitors' gallery at Dum Dum airport, waving goodbye to Shibani. It was a cold morning. The sky was overcast. She'd stood on the jet-bridge for a long time, waving and wiping tears. Then she'd turned and disappeared.

We never saw each other again.

Bob's father wasn't the only one who'd borrowed money from Sikander Khan. While almost no one ever paid him back, Mr. Chung had. In '89, he sold his shop and emigrated to Canada (instead of Hong Kong). And before leaving, he offered to repay the loans he'd taken from Sikander Khan. The man accepted only a fraction of the amount Mr. Chung owed him, saying the family would need the cash to start their new life in Canada.

Khan Furniture had shut down by then. Rashid had died years ago, and Kanu had returned to his village. Sikandar Khan had invested whatever he was left with in a few rickshaws, a dozen or so, which he rented daily for a few hundred rupees. He'd lost all his savings, and depended entirely on the money his rickshaw-pullers fetched him. Which they gradually stopped doing.

He passed away in '91. The local doctor, who wrote his death certificate, knew Dad. He told him that Sikander Khan had died of starvation.

***

Years passed. Bombay became Mumbai. Six years later, Calcutta became Kolkata. "When the name of a place changes, a bit of its character changes with it," Mr. Mahapatra used to say. He taught us history in XI and XII. Of all our teachers at St. Anthony's, I liked him the most. He didn't live long enough to know his own city would prove him right one day. Calcutta *had* changed. It wasn't what it used to be. But it was still my home—I didn't know any place better than this city. And no city could be more suitable for someone like me, a boring, potbellied, single Anglo-Indian accountant without any goal or ambition in life. I couldn't imagine living anywhere else. In '96, when Uncle Roger, Dad's younger brother, and his family moved to Australia, Mum and Dad had asked me to join them. They had a chance to migrate as well, but they didn't want to go. "We're too old," Mum had said. "But you should go. Unless you want to be the last Anglo-Indian living in Calcutta." "Why not?" I'd laughed, annoying her. "There'd still be plenty of people here, right?"

I'd moved to Uncle Roger's Elliot Road flat after they left, but kept going to the old neighborhood at least twice a week as long as Mum and Dad were alive. They'd stayed put in that dingy old place on Madan Street. After Mum's death in 2009 (Dad had gone five years earlier), I hardly ever went to the Chandni Chowk area. Most of the people I knew there had gone by then—either left the city, or died. Like Andy. He'd become a good musician and had a busy schedule of gigs, but drank too much. He died a year before Dad. Within three years, Mush was gone—a heart attack. He'd taken over his father's tailoring business and had been doing well. I never heard from Rustom and Bob. And no one knew where Bapi was, or whether he was even alive anymore.

So Raju and I were the only ones left. And we even managed to stay in touch, and see each other once or twice a year. Mostly around Christmas. He'd call and come over with a big plum cake from Nahoum's (our old favorite), and we'd have a drink at my place if he had the time. Raju was a busy man, the owner of a travel agency with offices everywhere, plus a big family with old parents, wife and three children.

Last Christmas, he brought me a DVD along with the cake. "Your Christmas gift, Bertie," he said, handing it to me. *Grand Trunk Road*, a Hindi film from the early 70s. "Call me when you're done watching it," he said, "and let's meet in January."

Sikandar Khan was in the film. In a song-and-dance scene, he smiles, holds the heroine's hand, runs half a circle with her, then letting go of her hand he gets out of the frame. Just a few brief moments. But *there he was!* I'd rewound and played that part many times to make sure I wasn't making a mistake.

It was Christmas Eve, around seven in the evening. I pressed *rewind* again, then pressed *pause*. *Silent Night* was playing on the radio somewhere. I went to the fridge and poured myself another beer. I imagined the faces of Andy, Mush and Bapi, and those of the rest of us, as we were all those years ago, in that lost life. I imagined us watching this together and being happy like we'd never been.

I took a gulp of beer and wiped my eyes dry. Then I pressed *play*.

RULES OF WAKING LIFE

Sarmishtha Tewari (Sasha), twenty-three years old
Profession: modeling
Place of recording: dreamer's home in Alipore, Kolkata
Date of dream: 14 April, 2003
Date of recording: 14 April, 2003

Ready? Can I start?

Yes.

Okay, recording....

For a long time, I didn't know who it was. Then it became clear...after a point...that it was the same person. Whoever it was. The same face. Not always, but mostly. And it would stare at me the same way. With a funny look. You know...like, it's trying to tell me something. Dream after dream, he'd show up and go away in the same manner. Just when you don't expect him to.

Do you *know* who it is?

Now I think I do. In fact, whenever I saw the face—not last night, but before—I sort of had the feeling that it was him. Although he didn't always look the same. Something about him would change depending on the dream. So there was no way I could know for sure if it was him. It's crazy. Anyway, what happened last night was this....

Long pause

I'm in my brother's house...but maybe not. It's just a place I think I know. I see my brother there, my sister-in-law. I see their son. And they behave like it's their home, so maybe it is. There are lots of other people there that I know. And two or three girls I used to know in school. I'd totally forgotten them...haven't seen them in years. Suddenly, they're in my dream, along with my friends and colleagues, as if they belong in the same group. And there are a few faces I don't know. I see all these people as I walk from one room to another. I don't know what they're doing in my brother's house. Maybe they're having a party or something. Maybe I'm in the party as well. I don't know. It's really crazy. And the place is not very well lit...so you can't see people clearly. And lots of things happen. Unrelated, crazy things. Like, there's this guy...sitting in a chair next to the phone. He's talking to someone...on the phone. I can't see his face, so I don't know who it is. But I know who he's talking to—I can hear the voice at the other end. It's *that* loud. Almost as if the speaker phone was on. But it wasn't, because the guy was holding the receiver, the handset. And the voice at the other end is my mother's. They're flirting. This guy and my mother. They're talking about...strange things. About...taking pictures, my mother posing for him in sexy clothes. You know? Stuff like that. And this guy turns out to be my friend Vir, although he looks like someone else. And I'm mad at my mother...because she's flirting with my friend. I snatch the handset from Vir, and tell my mother something like..."Ma, I've heard everything—shame on you! Wait till I tell Papa." And my mother says, completely unfazed, "Papa is right here, my dear. Want to talk to him?" And I'm so angry I don't know what to do. I start to cry.

Pause

Suddenly, in the middle of all this...this other guy comes running, and says his brother has died. Once again, it's someone I know. I know him very well, but I can't place him because he looks different. He talks about how his brother died. In detail. He says...he thinks his father had a hand in it. Something like that. Very strange! And I'm so horrified and sad, I don't want to listen to him anymore. But he goes on talking about it with a straight face. No emotions or anything! Strange things like that happen, one after another. Totally unrelated, but they overlap in a crazy way. And they have nothing to do with the party, although they happen right there, in my brother's house. And the party goes on....

Pause

Oh, and before this, before this crazy party—I should've started with this, because that's how the whole thing started last night—I'm at an official place. An embassy, or a consulate. Or a bank. I don't know. And the security is tight. I'm with someone I know...but I don't remember who it was. We're in a line, and suddenly she goes bonkers, and starts behaving like a crazy woman. She starts screaming at the top of her lungs, saying things like "Put your hands up," "don't move". And I'm scared as hell, trying to shut her up. "What are you doing? Stop!" I tell her. But she goes on...and then three or four big men, security guys, pounce on us. I'm crying and this woman, whoever she is, is laughing and saying, "It was just a joke. Just wanted to see if we could scare you. That's all." But by then we're handcuffed. And one of these men, whose face I remember, keeps staring at me with a dirty smile. He's big, dark...and with gray hair. He's pretending to frisk, and is touching me...smiling that way. It's creepy.

They don't talk to us. They just tie our wrists together. My left and her right. And we know that we're going to be detained. We won't be able to go home. And I panic.

Pause

Then we're in an empty room, which looks like a garage. The men leave us alone...but we know that they're coming back. We try desperately to undo the handcuff, wrenching our wrists against one another. It hurts like hell, and I start to cry. Then it suddenly comes loose. I slump to the floor, my back against the wall. The shutters aren't rolled down all the way, so there's a gap at the bottom. We crawl out through the gap. Then we're out on the street, and it's raining. We run for dear life. We're running...and I'm running faster than her. She keeps falling behind. And we look back over our shoulders to see if the men are behind us. Suddenly, there's a taxi in front us. I've never seen a yellow Ambassador taxi that is so long. It's huge. Like, you know, a stretch limousine. It's streaked with muddy rainwater, as if it was raining mud. There's mud all over it. It's, like, *yuk!* Really ugly. But we want it to stop, because we want to get into it. We're desperate. It's just ahead of us, cruising, but it doesn't stop....

Long pause

After that...I'm at this strange party, or whatever it was. And there are all these people doing God knows what. They're in groups of three or four, or five...hanging around, talking, laughing. And I'm walking from one room to another. I don't know what I'm doing that for...until it suddenly occurs to me that I'm looking for a glass of water. For my brother's son. So I'm walking around with an empty glass...looking for water. And there is of course no water. There's no water in the whole flat. I run into a small group of people I know very well—my friends, I don't remember exactly who all, but they seem pretty close to me. They ask me to sit down and talk. I tell them...that I'm looking for a glass of water for my nephew, my brother's son...and that I'll be with them in a minute. I ask them to wait for me, and I walk in and out of rooms. I'm going in through one door and coming out another. With an empty glass in my hand. In and out, in and out. It's crazy. And I cannot...find the damn kitchen, and it irritates the hell out of me. I want to join my friends, but I can't do that...until I get the water for my nephew. Then I'm in front of another room. And the door is closed. I push the door open; it's my brother's office, where he sees his patients. It even smells of medicine. You know? That funny smell...you get in a doctor's office? It's full of that. And it is darker than the rest of the place, so I switch on the light. God knows why I do that, because...obviously, I was not going to find water in that room. But, no...wait...I switch on the light because...I hear something. I hear strange noises. Like there are people there. So I want to see what's going on, and I turn on the light. As soon as I do that...I see...I can see....

Pause

Um, I find my ex-boyfriend. Naked. Lying on the table where my brother examines his patients. Can you imagine? With a woman...who is also naked. *God!*

Pause

Are you sure it was him?

Absolutely! Although...I can't see his face. It's hidden behind the woman's head...her hair. But it's *him*. The same...body. I recognize his jeans, his belt...with its big fat Hell's Angles buckle, his shirt—they are on a chair. And his shoes, which don't have his socks in them.

Because he has them on, his socks. *As usual!* Then there's the smell of his cologne...mixed with all the medicine smells. It *is* him! And he knows I'm in the room, but he doesn't stop. I rush out of the room, slamming the door shut. I forget about the water for my nephew. I look for my friends instead, because I want to tell them what a bastard my boyfriend is. But they're gone. All of them. And all the others, too. Suddenly, the whole house is empty. And I'm angry. I'm absolutely furious. I'm stomping around the whole place, and I don't know why I'm doing that. And there's no one there. Not even my brother and his wife. Or my nephew.

Pause

And guess what happens next? Guess who walks up to me? *You!* Out of the blue. There are little white things in your hair. As if it was snowing outside. Snow in Kolkata, right? I don't know how I got that. Anyway, I ask you where everybody is. You say...you say something funny...like..."They've gone to play holi." And I go, "What? It's the middle of the night, and it's snowing outside! How can they be playing holi?" And you say, "I didn't go with them because I wanted to tell you that I love you. But don't tell anyone!" That's the cutest thing that happens in the entire dream. Which was, like, a total khichdi. And a horrible one at that, too. And I think...you even give me a flower, which takes my heart away. And I brush the snowflakes from your hair, saying, "You know what? The son of a bitch is fucking another woman." That's what I say to you. Because I'm still angry....

Did you recognize the woman?

No. It could be...no, I'm not sure. I'm not sure. Then I woke up. And I was still angry. My heart was beating like crazy. And I couldn't go back to sleep for a long time.

I don't know why I was so angry. I broke up with him. What he does now is none of my business, right? It shouldn't matter to me anymore. Because *he* doesn't matter to me anymore. You know? But I was really, really angry. I stayed awake for a long time, thinking about the dream...and all the stupid things that happened in it. Including you...being romantic with me. Which was the best, I promise. When I fell asleep again, I had another dream. And it was even more weird. It was ugly! It was ugly as hell. Are you sure you want to hear this?

Yes.

Pause

Okay, let's do this quickly. Um...I don't remember how it starts. Some vague, stupid things happen...and I find myself in this huge space. It's like a...like an art gallery. Or something like that. A huge hall...a lobby, like inside a cinema hall—the space that leads to the actual auditorium. I'm sitting at a table...in a corner. And I'm talking to somebody. Not any *body*—there's no *body* there, just a head. *God!* And it has the face...that always stared at me in all those other dreams. You know? And the face keeps changing, too...from one look to another. As if it was changing masks. As if to remind me of all the different faces I've been seeing...in all those other dreams. Like, it was trying to tell me...that it's *him* that I've been seeing all this time. His face...in different forms. He's the one who's been appearing to me...in disguise. And it's my ex. It's *his* face. His head. Without the body. Sitting on the table itself. A cup of coffee in front of him—*it!* And he's talking to me...about God knows what. I cannot pay attention to what he's saying, because...I'm looking at his head sitting on the table. Can you believe it? I keep staring...at how his neck suddenly ends—all the muscles, veins and everything—how all these things suddenly end, and the wood of the table begins. I keep staring...in disbelief. And horror. I'm absolutely horrified! But cannot take my eyes off the place where his neck meets the table. And how seamless it is—how the flesh meets the wood. They even have the same color. The whole time, the face keeps changing. And talking.... And I want to leave. I want to run away. I push my chair back and stand up, starting to go. The head gets off the table, and follows me. Still talking, as if it was all very normal. There are a few people walking around the hall, but they don't pay any attention to me and...the head. As if it was all very normal. A woman followed by a talking head. Cool! Normal! I try to walk faster. But the head somehow manages to keep pace. I don't know how, because I don't look back, but I know it's just behind me. I can hear his voice—*its* voice, which starts to get angry. It starts shouting the way *he* always does. Or did. And I'm so scared I start running....

The maid's bell woke me up. You can't believe how happy I was...that it did. I was sweating like a pig. And I still can't get over the weirdness—the *ugliness*—of the whole thing! It's never been so bad before, so strange and horrifying. *So hideously bad!*

Pause

Okay, stop.

Recording stopped. Disclaimer: Sasha is a recent acquaintance. We're not close enough for me to appear in her dream the way she described. But if there's anything my hobby of collecting dreams has taught me, it's that dreams don't follow the rules of waking life.

HAMMER AND SICKLE

Tripti waited anxiously for the sun to set. She'd put on a sari Bikash liked to see her in. A hand-woven cotton Tangail with gray body and pale-blue borders. She'd washed, starched, and ironed it for today's visit. She was going to see him where she'd never seen him before.

They'd known each other for almost a year, but most of their meetings until then had been either in one of the narrow, poorly lit alleys of the neighborhood, or on the roof of a big, dilapidated house that belonged to one of her colleagues. Tripti would find pieces of paper slipped under her door with messages like *Lamp post no. 6, eight-15*, or *3rd lane, green door, seven-30*, or *Roof, six-30*—locations on their private map; only they knew where these places were. Sometimes, he would knock on the door, and step in for a few minutes only to let her know when and where they could meet next.

Tripti paced the rooms, glancing at her watch every now and then. When her legs tired, she sat down on the edge of her bed, and fanned herself with the day's newspaper. Or stood in front of the mirror, wiping her sweat-soaked face. For the last few days, the heat had been so intense it felt like a gummy, suffocating mass trapping everything inside it. There were newspaper reports of unprecedented water and power shortages caused by high temperatures across most of the state. *No Respite from the Heat in Sight,* read one headline today.

On the same page, there was a report Tripti had read so many times that she'd learned it by heart. The civil engineering professor from Jadavpur University, who'd been missing since last week, was now feared dead. The Naxals were blamed.

Tripti had met the man only a month ago at Mrs. Sen's house. Amala Sen, the headmistress of Krishna Mohan Girls' High School, where Tripti taught physics and chemistry to Class VII students. His name was Parthopratim Ganguly. He'd been talking heatedly to Mr. Sen about politics, and at one point said, "The Naxals are a nuisance. A menace to civil society. And the sooner we can get rid of them the better."

"How can you say that about people who are trying to ensure a better future for all?" Tripti had countered. "Including those who have nothing. Especially for them!"

"A better future for the poor by slaughtering professors and police constables, right?" he'd sneered at her. "That's how they're trying to ensure collective welfare, is that right, madam?"

"No, it is not! But what about the police? What are *they* doing?"

"Tit for tat! They don't have a choice. Of course, they're breaking the rules of engagement. It's obvious. They're dragging people out of their homes at night, shooting at sight, and using the most inhuman means of torture to extract information. They're even killing people in custody. *Of course*, it's not right. And if Charu Majumdar's gangs go on doing what they're doing in the name of revolution, class struggle, police violence will only get worse. I can assure you. And you can't blame the authorities. There's no other way to stop this nightmare of pipe guns and hand bombs!"

According to the report, undisclosed sources had confirmed that the Naxals, who regarded Parthopratim Ganguly as an ideological enemy, were behind his disappearance.

It was almost six by Tripti's watch when the heat finally eased a little. The sun was about to set. With another look in the mirror, hastily dabbing her face with the edge of her sari, she stepped out of the house.

The sweet shop, one of the grocery stores, the paan-and-cigarette stand, and the two tailoring shops were open, and so was the modest chamber of the homeopathic doctor. There were people on the street, but not nearly as many as one would have expected at that hour. A hot, tarry smell rose from the parts of the road where the asphalt still held the gravel together. The sweet shop owner, the paan-wallah, and the grocer had sprinkled water in front of their shops to keep the dust from flying. The smell rising from those patches of dampness reminded Tripti of the scent from the year's first rain.

Walking past the closed shutters of the jewelry shop, the owner of which had been killed by the Naxals because he was a police informer, she thought about the ghastly night she'd spent in her sister's house earlier in the summer. They were about to eat dinner when they heard hair-raising cries coming from the fields behind the government quarters on Golf Club Road. "I didn't do anything...please...let me go...I don't know them...please don't...please—" *Pfitt! Pfitt!* Sharp, echoless gunshots had silenced the voice, as Tripti, her sister and her eight-year-old son sat huddled in one room, barely breathing. Later in the night, they'd heard more howling voices, and more gunshots. There was no telling who was killing whom. It could have been the police shooting men they thought were Naxals. Or it could have been the Naxals eliminating their class enemies.

"Not right, not right!" Tripti had said to Bikash the next time they met. They were in an empty, dimly-lit lane behind the glass factory that had been closed for years. "What you're doing is not right. I may not understand politics, but revolution cannot be only about killing people!" "Stop!" Bikash had hissed, gripping her shoulders with both hands, and shaking her so hard that her back thudded against the wall behind her. She'd never seen him get so angry before. "Five of our comrades were killed on the golf course last week. It was *them* you'd heard begging for their lives. So please shut up!"

Coming up to the hyacinth-choked pond, where they said the jeweler's body had been found, she slipped into an alley on her left. There were fewer people on this narrow, unpaved lane, which wound through a residential area full of old trees, mostly neem, mango, rose apple, guava, and palm, and ancient, dilapidated houses. Open earth drains with black, algae-thickened water on both sides of the lane gave off a pungent rotten-sweet odor. Grass and weeds sprouted randomly along their soft, soggy edges. An uneven bed of broken bricks lay where the path dipped near a puddle rimmed with wild arums between the fences of two relatively new houses. The fetid stench was stronger here. To avoid the smell, Tripti quickened her step and stumbled on a piece of brick. Relieved that she was unhurt, she walked more watchfully now.

The sound of a news bulletin reached her ears. It was coming out of a hut made of bamboo splits and tin, which stood a few feet behind a sparse, badly neglected hedge. The windows were shut. Apart from the radio sound, there was nothing to suggest there was anyone inside. *Who would keep their windows closed at this hour?* she thought, wondering if it was another hideout for Bikash and his comrades, or their rivals. Or police informers. The inertness of the air around the hut seemed ominous.

Tripti turned her eyes back to the path. It was empty. Then, a little distance ahead of her, a young boy came running out of a gate, followed by an older girl. Giggling breathlessly, they ran a few meters down the lane, one trailing the other, and then disappeared behind a rickety fence on the other side. The little ripple of their panting laughter and running feet sank back into the stillness as quickly as it had surfaced. Tripti's thoughts went back to the hut she'd just passed. Imagining the heat trapped under that tin roof, she became aware of how profusely she'd been sweating. The gluey moisture clung to her arms like a pair of long, transparent, skin-tight sleeves. Picking up the edge of her sari, she dabbed her cheeks and throat, the nape of her neck, and the sides of her forehead, and then pressed it against her palms and forearms. The armpits and back of her blouse were wet.

Darkness, clotted wisps of the approaching night, had started to collect like flotsam among the middle and lower branches of the big mango and neem trees. Above their upper boughs, and the straggling palm fronds, the sky was a frayed patchwork of electric orange-blue. The sound of a few conch shells bellowed pensively in the jellylike, charcoal-green dome of warm, stagnant air.

Tripti shuffled along, holding her pace at an inconspicuous level between a leisurely stroll and a purposeful march.

She'd been begging Bikash for a long time to let her come to his hideout. "Just once," she would plead, "and I won't stay long." But he would shake his head and say, "Not safe for you. Or for me and my boys. And you won't know anything more about me if you see me there." But that was hardly the reason why she'd wanted to come. She'd already known the man well enough. There was nothing she didn't know that a trip to his hideout was going to reveal. She'd just been anxious to see the place, the four walls and the roof that sheltered him, to find out for herself if the place was really safe. That was all.

It was on his eleventh visit he'd finally disclosed his name to Tripti. Until then, every time he knocked on the door and she asked, "Who is it?" he'd reply with a gentle *Me*. The voice was unmistakable. The deep, unhurried sound it generated had the solidity of a mountain. It was so dense it seemed almost visible, occupying an expanse of physical space in front of her. A space that felt like it could shelter her forever. *Me*. Bikash Ganguly. A small man, though. Scrawny and bearded, with unkempt hair and lips gone dark from years of smoking.

Tripti's heart started to beat faster as she approached the boundary wall of the old mansion that had been turned into a mental asylum. At the farthest end of the wall, where the lane crossed another, a boy on a bicycle would wait by a lamp post. He would show her the way, riding ahead of her. Then he would get off the bicycle in front of a house, pretending to check the tires.

In a few minutes, Tripti was where the boy had stopped. It was not the house he'd faced, but the one he had his back to.

Flanked by vacant plots overrun with dense thickets and wild vines, it was an unremarkable building with a courtyard full of trees. Pink cascades of bougainvillea hung above a gate of unpainted, rusting steel at the end of a long, chest-high brick wall. Shards of glass were embedded all along the wall's cement-topped ridge. One of the pillars that held the gate, the one on Tripti's right, as she stood facing it, had a small wooden letterbox nailed to it. It hung askew, without any number or name that she could see.

Apart from the routine noise of crows returning to their evening roosts, the occasional barking of a dog, the sound of a radio, a crying child, a conch shell or a bell, Tripti couldn't hear anything. The taut silence that surrounded the house reminded her of that bamboo-and-tin hut with closed windows.

She paused for a few moments, hesitating, not daring to look in any direction to see if she was being watched. Then, as she started to open the gate, tentatively, almost fearfully, a disconcerting thought crossed her mind. *What if it was a trap?* Like the one they'd laid for Sandhya Banik, a girl Tripti used to know. Her mutilated body had been found in an abandoned house in Garia. They said she'd been lured into that place by the false prospect of meeting her friend, an active Naxal cadre like Bikash.

There was movement at the far end of the bow-shaped pathway that led to the building. A sudden stir in the stillness—a flash of white, dull white, persistent patches of it, through the dark filigree of foliage. It followed the arc of the passage, with a gentle rise and fall, in her direction.

Tripti froze, a hand resting on the gate.

"Come." Bikash stood, apathetic, unsmiling, at the bend of the path, in full view. In a crumpled, off-white khadi Punjabi, sleeves pushed up to his elbows, dirty-green pants and blue rubber slippers. Tripti had rarely seen him wear anything else. "Come in," he said again in a hushed voice, with a slight nod, and then turned and started to walk back.

With a mixture of apprehension and a mysterious, bone-chilling fear, Tripti followed. Slowly at first, and then quickened her step to catch up to him as they got close to the house. Climbing the steps to the verandah, she drew level and walked alongside him. The entrance to the house was at one end of a U-shaped corridor behind the courtyard's lush vegetation. Rooms with closed doors lined the passage. At the foot of one door, which was slightly ajar, flies were whining above what in that half-light looked like thick pools of some liquid.

"What is that?" she whispered.

"Nothing," Bikash promptly replied, throwing a quick brooding glance back at the entrance. He pulled the door shut and bolted it, and then said, "Fish blood. The boys forgot to clean up." Without another word, he led Tripti to a room at the other end of the corridor.

It was a small room without a window, filled with the smell of biri and something Tripti couldn't quite place. The ceiling was low, its edges and corners blotched with thin fog-patches of cobwebs. In the one just above her head, she spotted a dead spider. A single naked lamp hung from above the doorframe. At one end of the room Tripti noticed a closed door, which looked new, purpose-built, and smaller than usual. Next to it, against the wall, was an ordinary wooden cot with a thin, badly stained mattress rolled up on it, and newspapers, books, and grocery bags underneath. *So this is where he sleeps!* she thought. A table with two chairs, and a rickety bookcase crammed with books and propaganda material—bundles of handbills, small posters, paper flags—stood at the other end of the room. At the foot of the bookcase, a thick sheaf of newspaper-size posters lay on the floor, covered partly by a loose roll of red cotton banners.

"Sit," Bikash said, closing the door. He went around the small table to sit in the chair on the other side. "Tea?" A black-and-white picture of Mao Tse-tung hung on the unpainted wall behind him, and next to it a calendar with dates marked in red.

"No," Tripti said. "Isn't that Charu Majumdar?" She was looking at a booklet lying on the table, a cheaply produced party manifesto. The picture on the cover was half-hidden under a paperweight of chipped green glass.

"Yes." He lit a biri and leaned back in his chair. He puffed thoughtfully for a few moments. Then, exhaling a slow jet of smoke, he said, with a fine gray plume still coming out of his mouth in small bursts, "Was it difficult?"

"What?" Her mind was on the paperweight. She was wondering what its role could be in a room without either windows or a fan.

"Coming here?"

"No." Tripti shook her head. "It wasn't difficult. Not at all." She smiled reassuringly. "I know the area. Not every lane and by-lane, of course. Like you." She paused, expecting him to say something. "But I have an idea," she continued a moment later. "A distant relative of mine, an old aunt, used to live here. Not exactly here, but close by. Not far from the big mansion."

"The asylum."

"Right. The corner where I met your boy. But in the opposite direction."

Bikash nodded. He picked up the matchbox from the table to relight the biri, which had gone out.

"But finding the house...without him—" Footfalls in the corridor distracted Tripti. She shook her head absently for a brief moment, and then lowering her voice added, "I couldn't have found it."

"No name, no number." A thin smile crossed his face, unmoved by the sound of activity outside—doors opening and closing, something being dragged along the floor, hushed voices.

"And it doesn't look very different from other houses in this lane!"

But inside, it was a different world. A world ruled by the hammer and sickle—CPI (ML), red flag, revolution! It was a world about changing things, about getting rid of whatever came in the way of change, or whoever— politicians, policemen, landlords, teachers. Tripti thought about the missing professor: *The Naxals are a nuisance. A menace to civil society.* She wondered if Bikash had read the news. If she were to mention it, it would be hard to hide the fact that she'd met the man. She hadn't told him anything about that evening at Mrs. Sen's house.

Tripti stared at him—his thin, inscrutable face. There was a calmness in his large eyes that often sent shivers down her spine. Nothing seemed to ruffle that, not even when he talked about the most gruesome things. The slaughter of his comrades, or the brutality he suffered at the hands of the police. She remembered the Beniapukur Police Station episode, "the toughest endurance test so far," as he'd put it. But when he talked about it, there was nothing in his appearance to suggest that that indeed had been the case. They'd bent his fingers backward, breaking two in his right hand and one in his left, and stuck needles under his nails. He'd been hung upside down and thrashed until he fainted. He'd given Tripti those details as placidly as he would have talked about a trip to the local bazaar. "If they find me again, they won't bother putting me in jail," he'd said with an unsettling casualness. "They'll just finish me off."

Those fingers! "Can I see your hand?" Tripti reached across the table.

"Don't tell me you're into palmistry?" Bikash dropped his biri in an earthen teacup-turned-ashtray and held out his right hand.

"I'm not," she said. "The other one, too."

Long, sturdy fingers for a small man, except those three, which with their knotted inscription of pain looked thin and weak. Tripti let his palms rest on one of hers, and with the other gently stroked the broken fingers. She lifted them to her face and inhaled their intoxicating aroma—a mixture of biri, old books, and Boroline (Boroline because he'd cut one of his knuckles). She filled her lungs as fully as she could with the smell, which reminded her, on that sweltering summer evening, of burning winter leaves and faraway places.

"Tripti," Bikash said, retrieving one of his hands. "Listen. We need to wrap up."

"What? Why?"

"It's not a good day. I couldn't send a message in time to ask you not to come. But it's not a good day."

"Why?"

He smiled. "You don't need to know that. But you should go."

She raised his other hand, which she still had in her grip, back to her face, clutching it more tightly.

He rose from his chair, and came and stood next to hers. He put the free hand on the back of her head. "Some other time, Tripti. I'll let you know."

The roll of her long, oil-quenched hair came undone. "Five minutes, please?" she pleaded, lifting her face from his palm.

A schoolteacher in a Naxal's den, kissing a hand that killed, and would likely kill again. But she didn't care.

Bikash's face glistened in the airless heat as he stared down at her.

Tripti, still holding his hand, pressed it against her sweaty, heaving breasts. She tugged at the shoulder of his Punjabi, not caring if the cloth tore, to pull his face down to hers. The only thing that could stop her then, as it had countless times before, was fear, the insufferable fear of consequence. But that, for the first time in her life, to her own amazement, she'd triumphed over completely for a few heart-racing moments.

She dragged him to his bed, and forced him down on the rolled-up mattress with a boldness and strength she'd never thought she possessed.

"Whoever discovers the who of me will find out the who of you," he whispered as she stood adjusting her sari a few minutes later. They heard hushed voices outside.

"And the why, and the where." He paused and smiled. "A Latin American poet said that. Maybe about two people just like us."

Tripti stepped closer to him, trying to throw her arms around his neck.

Bikash stepped back, holding out a hand. "You have to leave now. Please!"

The door was open when she walked past it on her way out of the house. Despite a strange foreboding, she couldn't resist a quick glance, but couldn't see anything inside the unlit room. A salty smell had replaced the swarm of flies.

A cycle-van stood in the courtyard. It was parked in the open space to the right of the steps coming down from the verandah. Walking past the cart, she saw, in the light that came out of a part of the house, a heap of damp gunnysacks.

"Stop!" An intimidating voice startled Tripti. "Who are you?" A tall man loomed in the passage behind the parapet, coming closer. He wasn't more than seven or eight feet away, but she couldn't see the face clearly.

"It's okay, let her go," someone else said from some other part of the house. It wasn't Bikash.

With fearful hesitation, she turned to resume her walk, expecting to hear something else. Or see someone, or to be stopped again. But when nothing happened in the next few seconds, and she was close to where the path curved, about to be hidden behind the bank of ghostly foliage, she started to walk at a normal pace. A thin shaft of light from somewhere lit up a single bunch of bougainvillea above the gate.

Once outside, Tripti closed the gate behind her without any noise, putting the latch back down softly. Then, without looking back even once, she hurried home, wondering how many people in that house knew her, and knew that she was there. But neither that, nor the fact that Bikash never noticed her sari, seemed to matter.

"Whoever discovers the who of me...," she muttered under her breath. "And the why...and the where."

FIFTEEN DAYS

For fifteen days in a row, Zoya hasn't said a word about death or dying. This is the longest lull since the problem started five months ago. There have been periods of quiet before, the longer ones usually stretching to five or six days. A week at the most, not more than that. Now fifteen days! It's a miracle, although we're not sure how long it will last.

Zoya is my only child. She's almost six, and like any single child of a single mother, thinks her mother—this five-foot-seven, sixty-one kilo shapeless center of her tiny universe—can solve all the riddles of life. And answer all her questions: *Why did Daddy leave us? Will you also die like Nani* (my mother)*? Why do Ramu and Laxmi and their mother sleep on the road? Where will they go if it starts to rain?*

"Daddy" is my ex-husband Zubin. A man with a heart of gold, and with so much patience and such incredible tolerance for nonsense, that even Mr. Singh's noisy, foul-mouthed parrot couldn't get him angry when we were living in his Moira Street flat. Mr. Singh lived next door. He was a retired music teacher, and the bird was his only companion. It sat in a cage just outside our bedroom window and screamed *Who the fuck is that?* every time it heard something. *Shut up, you junglee bastard!* And then it sang *Knock, knock, knocking on heaven's door.* It did that all day long. The weekdays were fine, because we were not at home the whole day, but the weekends were a nightmare. Zubin laughed every time he heard the bird, and begged me not to say anything to Mr. Singh. "The bird is all he has, the poor man," he'd say.

There were countless other proofs of his kindness, but as a husband...well, *a disaster* would be putting it mildly. He didn't have the slightest clue about the role, about what it meant to be a husband. The whole time we were together, he behaved like, *so what he was married?* he could carry on minding his own business the way he always had. He didn't know how to inhabit the space next to the woman he was living with, make it at least halfway full, as a partner. As a *married* man. He had no intuition or drive for that. I still wonder how I could've overlooked this gaping hole in him when we were seeing each other. How could it take so long to realize that Zubin was a top-notch corporate professional, a good neighbor, a caring friend, but *not* a family man. Not even a good father!

Zoya is obsessed with death. Not just with the idea and the fact of it—that every living thing dies, and everyone she knows, including herself, will die one day— but also with the ways in which it can happen. Violent, painful, gruesome ways. Like accidents—people getting run over by buses and trucks, or falling from tall buildings. Limbs getting cut off. I have no idea what triggered all this in her. Zubin thinks it's something she watched on TV. He blames it on Cartoon Network.

It all started just before Christmas last year. She came home from school one day and started talking about Jesus. Miss Sen, their English teacher, had told them stories about Christmas, stories she'd heard countless times before. "Mama, did Jesus cry when they put him on the cross?" she asked. "Those nails?" She held up her left hand, the right forefinger in the middle of the palm.

"Zoya, Christmas is about his birth," I said. "Why are we talking about the cross? Did Miss Sen say anything about it?"

"No." She shook her head.

"Then?"

She walked away, distracted, saying she needed to go to the toilet.

The next day, I was tucking her into bed when she started to cry. Suddenly! Lips pressed tight, face twisted and her body jerking like she wasn't a child but a woman in labor. It reminded me of when I was giving birth to her. "What happened?" I asked, scared that something terrible must have happened inside this small fragile body of hers. "Is your belly hurting? Did you hurt yourself in school today? Do you want me to call the doctor?"

She shook her head. "The nails," she said through her racking sobs.

That's how it started. At least that's when I noticed it for the first time. Jesus and his crucifixion kept coming up. Which is odd because we're not even Christian, like most families who send their kids to Carmel Primary School. The subject carries no additional meaning for us.

I was convinced that it was all the crosses and the pictures of Jesus she sees in school that had started this nightmare. Then this happens: Zoya and I are lying on the sofa on a Sunday morning after breakfast. Now that Christmas is behind us, we're talking about what we'll do on New Year's Eve, which is only a day away. We're invited to two of my colleagues—Malavika (she and I have been grinding away together as ticket agents for years), and Vikram, our head of sales at the city office. Both have children who are roughly Zoya's age, and we cannot decide whether to go to both places or choose one.

"Look," I say, "we'll have to be back home by nine because JD will wait for us." JD is short for Jogen Das, a former colleague who's fast becoming the second light of my life, after Zoya. He spends three or four days a week in our flat, and is now thinking of moving in permanently. "So maybe we should only visit Malavika Auntie?" I suggest. "So that we don't get late?"

Zoya is holding my right hand in both of hers, her head resting against my right shoulder. "Mama?"

"Yes?"

"Mama?"

"Go on, Zoya, I'm listening. What is it?"

"If your hand...."

"Yeah? What about it?"

"If it gets cut off...," she pauses.

"What?"

"If your hand gets cut off....will it die...alone? Before you do?"

We wound up staying at home on New Year's Eve. I texted Malavika and Vikram saying I couldn't come because I was a bit unwell. I was, in fact, far worse.

"Oh, Seema...Seema," JD sighed, putting the takeaway boxes from Mocambo on the table—matar paneer, chana masala, dal makhani, stuffed tandoori chicken, peas pulao and naan—my favorite dishes all, but today I had no appetite for any of them. He put the plastic bag in the bin and washed his hands in the kitchen sink. "There's no reason for you to be so worked up about it just yet." He shook his head reassuringly, looking me in the eye, drying his hands. "Let Ghoshal Uncle talk to her and tell us what he thinks. He's the best child psychologist we have here, believe me. And I'm not saying this because he's a family friend. The guy's good." Stepping closer, JD put his arms around my shoulders, the kitchen towel still in his hand. "Seema," he said. The smell of food made my stomach turn. He pressed his lips to mine.

"You smell of beer," I said, stepping back.

"Had one while waiting for the food," he said half apologetically. "Do you want one?"

"Maybe a gin."

He made me one with tonic water, a slice of lime, and a lot of ice. I like it with a lot of ice. I finished it in three or four gulps. It was a few minutes past eight, still too early for Zoya to be ready for bed. Plus, it was the New Year's Eve. If we'd gone to either Malavika's or Vikram's, we wouldn't be back yet. She was watching *Dora, The Explorer* on DVD.

After the second drink, which I had more slowly, I fed Zoya—she ate a bit of peas pulao and a few pieces of paneer—and got her ready for bed. "Good night, my angel," I whispered, pulling the duvet up to her chin and smoothing it down with both hands. Switching off her bedside lamp, I felt tears welling up in my eyes. "Happy New Year, Zoya," I said.

"Happy New Year, Mama," she cooed. Then, as I was walking away from her bed, she said, "Mama?"

"Yes?" I paused at the door, glad she couldn't see my face. Her room was dark and the light from the living room was behind me.

"Big girls don't cry."

"No, they don't," I said, somehow suppressing a howl. "You're right. Sleep tight, baby!"

JD had laid the table for the two of us—the food out of the takeaway boxes and into appropriate bowls, each with a serving spoon in it, plates and glasses, forks, knives, spoons, and paper napkins. A half-finished bottle of Bombay Sapphire, a plate of sliced lime. And between our two plates, in the middle of the table, a candle. I couldn't help thinking that my ex had *never* done anything like that.

"What we're doing here…," he paused, twisting the ice tray to get a few more cubes into my glass.

I waited as he finished getting my gin ready. He was drinking beer.

"What's happening…." He handed me the drink and sat down. "Is that…I'm not sure, of course…not an expert…but it seems to me that…that this is what Ghoshal Uncle would call catastrophizing."

I was looking at his face. He's so good-looking it's scary. When his eyes moved to the food on his plate, or when he reached for his glass of beer, I kept looking. It felt a little strange—looking at him when *he* wasn't looking at me. Like I was overstepping some boundary, intruding into a space I hadn't been granted access to. I thought about how all the female members on the staff had fallen for JD when he joined the company. There wasn't a single woman who didn't have a crush on him. Except me, of course. And that was not only because I was still married to Zubin, but also because I was too busy looking for a way out of the suffocating cage my relationship with Zubin had become. And being interested in another man didn't seem like the right way out. Even when the man was someone like JD, who, besides being so insanely attractive, was also quite approachable. I wasn't interested in anything that could lead to another emotional incarceration.

"Maybe you've never heard a child say what Zoya does—"

"Have you?" I asked without letting him finish.

"I can't tell you if I have or not. Maybe I haven't. But the point is...that doesn't mean anything. I mean, it doesn't necessarily mean that...it's a problem. The fact that she says what she does sometimes." He took a gulp of beer. "All I'm saying is let's not jump to conclusions. Let's wait until the expert tells us what it is. And meanwhile...." JD paused.

I remembered what Malavika used to say about him. *Take the face of Omar Sharif,* she'd say, gesturing as if she was holding it in her right hand, *the Omar Sharif of Dr. Zhivago, minus the mustache, and plop it onto Robert Redford's.* She'd put the right hand on top of her left with a clapping sound. *Darken the mix a bit and what you get is Jogen Das.* She was dead right. And she had a thing for him, too. "And meanwhile what?" I asked.

He lowered his head to put some food in his mouth. The candle's flame shone like a third eye in the middle of his forehead. Then he turned to pick up his glass of beer, the tip of the flame dancing menacingly below the lower lid of his right eye. As if it was aiming for the eye and would reach it any moment. A chill ran down my spine. I moved my chair to the right so that the candle was no longer in the middle.

"How about eating?" He caught me staring at him. "You haven't touched your food."

"Not hungry yet." I smiled.

"You shouldn't be drinking on an empty stomach."

I ate a few scraps of naan with I forget what, and had a few more drinks. By the time it was midnight, my head was like a whirlpool with a constantly changing center of gravity.

JD came around to my side of the table. Holding my face in both hands, he kissed me. "Happy New Year," he whispered, a riot of tandoori chicken, onion and beer on his breath.

"Happy New Year."

I smiled as tears rolled down my face.

The sound of the fireworks outside was a continuous rumble punctuated every now and then by a deafening blast close to the house. I feared Zoya might wake up, but she didn't. JD took me by the hand and led me to the window overlooking the street. He pulled the curtain to one side. The sky looked like an animated burst bouquet. Like it had on that Diwali night five years ago. I'd come here to visit Ammi. She'd gone downstairs for a Diwali get-together, so I was alone at home with Zoya, who was not yet a year old. I'd stood exactly where I was standing now, holding her in my arms, the back of my right hand touching the cold marble ledge. The window was closed but the sight of the street below through the clear glass had sent a violent shiver down my spine. The height—the distance between where I was and the ground! *What if I...?*

I'd slumped down on the floor, holding Zoya tightly, paralyzed by the worst possible fear. I'd stayed that way for a long time, my back to the window, not daring to stand up, until Ammi rang the bell. After that, I'd never stood here with Zoya in my arms.

"I want to go to bed," I said to JD.

Although the thought of divorce had been in my mind for a while, getting more and more well-defined as the days, weeks, and months went by, letting it out—letting Zubin know that—wasn't easy. *You know, Zubin, I think it's best if...I think, um...we tried our best, but... for our own sake...and for the sake of Zoya....* I kept rehearsing the lines in my head, speaking them out loud when I was alone. But no matter how I arranged the words, each string of them had this awful ring to it, stoking nothing but guilt in me. Plus, when was the right time to bring up the subject? Our marriage was bland and lackluster, but that also meant that you couldn't really find moments in it that were truly unpleasant. Moments that could give you the excuse—make you angry enough to say, *That's it, enough!*

Then there were the worries about Zoya, who was besotted with her father. Although he hardly spent any time with her, she always pretended to be playing with him if he was around. It didn't matter that he rarely responded to what she said or did. He just had to be there for her to come up with these elaborate make-believe games, which were so one-sided it was heartbreaking to watch them. But *she* was fine. She was happy! So I worried how our divorce might affect her.

Ammi was still around when I'd started to have these thoughts, which worried her. "No, Seema, no!" she said to me. "Don't do that. For *her* sake. No one is perfect. At least he's a good man!"

I didn't want to argue with her, but it didn't mean much to me—that he was a good man. Not anymore. If anything, I felt suffocated by that sterile, unmoving I'm-such-a-good-guy air about him. Even when he sensed that I was drifting away, his behavior didn't change.

It was around this time that Mr. Singh had lost his parrot. Zubin paid him several visits, and at home talked about how sad he was that the bird had died. And I thought, *So the death of your neighbor's pet is more important to you than the death of your own marriage?* I didn't tell him that, of course, but that's how I felt. He behaved like his feelings for me and Zoya weren't any different from what he felt for Mr. Singh. Or even that stupid bird! And the irony was that it was exactly this side of his personality that had attracted me to him—that he was equally good to everyone.

Funny how things change. Or don't. Zubin remained the man he'd been when we were still dating. He treated domestic life, which for him now included a wife and a child, as though its demands weren't any different from those of a candlelight dinner at a fine restaurant. As though all were good as long as he was courteous, had a good time himself, picked up the check at the end and left a generous tip. It was not up to him to worry about how the table had been laid or the food cooked. He was the guest. Never mind that it was his own flat that we were living in.

"I haven't been the mother I *can* be," I'd said to Ammi. "I'm too unhappy. I have to leave him someday. Before it's too late. I have to do that for Zoya's sake!"

Zubin had moved back to Bombay. He hadn't seen his daughter since last August. And I wasn't so keen on calling him about the stuff she'd been talking about, but JD said, "No matter what it is, he needs to know."

It was the beginning of the second week of January. Zoya's school had reopened. My anxieties about her had worsened over past couple of weeks, making my start into the new year the shakiest I'd ever had.

Zubin answered promptly even though he was at work. "Seema, what a surprise!" he said cheerfully. "Happy New Year once again!" He'd sent a message on the 31st with his good wishes and an ecard for me and Zoya. "What's up?"

"Do you have a few minutes?" I said.

I told him everything in as much detail as my memory permitted. Pointing out somewhere in the middle that I didn't expect him to do anything about it, but thought it was important that he knew. He needed to know the phase his daughter was in.

When I was done, he said, "Look, I think you're reading too much into it. Kids her age have all kinds of thoughts and ideas. They're finding out about things—life, death, dying—all kinds of things. Right? And it's not easy. And then they watch stuff on the TV. Who knows what *that* does to their young minds? I mean the stuff they see in newspapers and magazines or on the screen—it can definitely color their imagination. Make them think and imagine in ways you and I didn't when we were kids. Because all we had back then were books, right? Comic books, yes, but books! None of this audiovisual stuff."

"Well, comic books can also color your imagination, can't they?" I said meekly.

"Sure. But not like today's audiovisual media. Have you seen how violent some of these animation films are? They should stop airing them on channels like Cartoon Network."

"But...disembodied hands...on Cartoon Network?"

"Ah, that!" Zubin laughed. "But that was a good question, wasn't it? Will the hand die alone? Wow! Quite philosophical, if you ask me. I'd be impressed by the question...coming from a six-year-old. Not alarmed."

Two weeks later, we got our first appointment with Dr. Ghoshal. Zoya wanted to know why we were going to see a doctor. And why *all* three of us were going.

"He's a childhood friend of JD's father," I told her. "He calls him Ghoshal Uncle. He wants to meet us."

"Then why don't we invite him to our house?"

"Yes—"

"Are we going to his house?"

"We're going to his office. And yes, of course, we'll invite him once we get to know him. We'll do that for sure. And also...he wants to talk to you."

"Me? About what?"

"The things you talk to me about. You know, like...Jesus."

Zoya shrugged her dainty shoulders and instantly resumed her conversation with the stuffed toys propped against the armrest of the sofa.

It was a cold, gloomy day when we went to see Dr. Ghoshal. Both the light and the temperature seemed somewhat unusual for a late-January day in Calcutta. Almost matching the unusual nature of what we were doing—taking Zoya to a child psychologist.

After JD introduced me and Zoya to Dr. Ghoshal, he continued talking to us as if we'd really just dropped in to say hello. He talked about how JD's father and he had been best friends since they were in primary school. "No one in the world was as close to me as his father," he said. "Not even any of my siblings." He talked about their boyhood dreams and how they changed every two years. He asked me if my job was a dream-come-true for me.

"I wanted to be a lawyer," I told him.

"And I wanted to be a pilot," he laughed. "I mean, I wanted to be many things, but being a pilot was a wish that stayed with me the longest. And I don't know if you know…you may not," he glanced at JD, "but Jogen wanted to be a psychologist."

"I didn't know that," I said, looking at JD.

"I just wanted to copy my hero," he laughed, pointing at Dr. Ghoshal.

Zoya had got up from her chair in the meantime and walked over to a sideboard on the other side of the room. There were a few toys lying on the sideboard. She stood there looking at them.

"Zoya, do you like them?" Dr. Ghoshal said.

She nodded.

"Then you'll like what's in there. Go take a look."

After she'd walked in to the other room, Dr. Ghoshal stood up. "About twenty minutes, I'd say," he said softly. He picked up one of the toys from the sideboard, entered the room and gently closed the door behind him.

My heart started to race. It was as if my life itself was hanging in the balance.

Everything seemed to depend on what this man was going to say about my daughter. *Maybe it's all because of our divorce!* I hadn't grown up believing in prayers and didn't know any. But, in my mind, I kept saying, *Please, please, please, please don't let this happen to her.* I had no idea who I was saying this to. Maybe to Ammi and Appu, my only gods, who were dead. As if being dead had given them the power to protect Zoya in a way I couldn't. He'd gone before I started to work. I'd just finished college and the life ahead seemed to shimmer with possibilities, when he suddenly died. And Ammi died when Zoya turned four—two and a half months after her fourth birthday. I remembered Ammi's face every time she held Zoya in her arms. "My little Zoya Jeejee," she'd coo. She loved calling her that, dropping the last bit of Zubin's family name Jeejeebhoy. I'd never seen her face shine the way it did when she was near her granddaughter. *Please, Ammi, don't let this happen to your Zoya Jeejee,* I heard myself saying under my breath. *I'm sorry I didn't listen to you. My fault. My fault!*

On the wall behind us, a clock ticked loudly. My right hand felt clammy. I realized JD was holding it. He gave it a squeeze and let go of it as Dr. Ghoshal walked in.

Dr. Ghoshal told Zoya she could stay in the room and continue playing. He left the door open and came and sat in his chair. "So," he said. He threw quick glances at both of us and smiled. When neither of us said anything—I was too full of anxiety to ask any question, and maybe JD just wanted to hear the doctor talk—he began, "Okay, so...it seems to me that she doesn't have any deficits in terms of...empathy, the ability to bond with others, the ability to experience feelings adequately and express them, etc. These are some of the basic things you'd look at when you're trying to understand a child's behavior...and see if there's any problem there." He paused. "And there doesn't seem to be any as far as I could see. As for the thoughts...." He paused again. "Well, she mentioned Jesus. And the cross, the nails, etc. These thoughts seem to recur from time to time. And she doesn't like them."

"Did she say anything about...someone's hand getting cut off?" I asked.

"No, she didn't." Dr. Ghoshal shook his head. Then he said, "We all have thoughts popping into our heads now and then that we don't like. Unpleasant thoughts. Scary thoughts. They're products of our alarm system.

One of the brain's many ways of keeping us safe. So that we stay away from harmful things, sharp objects. Knives, nails, etc. So, having these thoughts is hardly unusual. What we have to see is how frequently she's having them. And are they so intrusive that her normal life is affected? That's the key question."

Zoya walked back into the room looking like she had a good time doing whatever she'd been doing.

"So, Zoya," Dr. Ghoshal said, turning to her. "Do you want to play that fun game again?"

Zoya nodded with a shy smile.

"Brilliant! Let's do it next week, then. Okay?" He turned back to us and smiled. "Same time next week?"

JD and I looked at each other and nodded.

"Yes," I said.

As he walked us to the door, he said, "Bring her next week and maybe one more time. That should be enough."

Apart from the roughly three and a half years of my married life with Zubin, which I spent in his flat on Moira Street, I'd never left this old apartment of ours in Ballygunge Park. I was Zoya's age when we moved here. This 1800-square-foot, three-bedroom unit on the 5th floor of an apartment house that had just been built. It was our own place—the only place we'd ever owned –and we were proud of it. We'd spent the happiest years of our lives here. And in the unhappy times—when Ammi and I lost Appu, and when Zoya and I lost Ammi—being here had given us solace. It was as if, as long as we were here, we weren't cut off from the part of life in which Appu and Ammi were alive. They'd occupied this exact same space, and being here gave us a tangible sense of continuity. A sense that what we'd lost wasn't entirely lost after all.

Zubin had continued to visit Zoya here until he moved back to Bombay last August. And JD started spending more time with us almost as soon as Zubin left Calcutta. It was obviously because of Zoya, although he never said so. He'd been worrying about how she might react to not seeing her father for months at a time. And the possible psychological effect of such a prolonged absence of one parent. He started going to ridiculous lengths to entertain Zoya. He'd spend hours doing up the dollhouse with her, play with her stuffed toys and pretend he was one of them. He'd ask her about her school, her friends (the names of whom he'd learned by heart) and listen to her attentively. He'd read her stories, play hide and seek with her, do silly dances on the floor, sing silly songs—none of which Zubin had ever done. None of which I'd ever expected JD to do. But there he was, he'd created a role for himself almost overnight, and completely voluntarily, without the slightest hint or suggestion from me or anyone else. And he fit it to a T.

Now he's showing signs that my worries about Zoya might have spread to his mind too. How does that make me feel? Relieved, of course—at least to an extent. A sudden lightening of the emotional load, now that there's another soul willing to carry some of it. But it hasn't come without a price tag of guilt. I feel like I've put on his shoulders a burden that wasn't his—was never meant to be. And I haven't done it out of anything more glorious than just a selfish need of emotional relief.

His thoughts about what needs to be done about her have changed since our second appointment with Dr. Ghoshal, which I thought had gone as well as the first, but somehow JD wasn't quite satisfied. "Shouldn't we consider talk therapy?" he'd asked the doctor. "Maybe five or six formal sessions?" But Dr. Ghoshal didn't agree, saying there wasn't any clear goal to set for such a process with Zoya. "What she has is not really a problem," he said. "But she hasn't stopped having those thoughts," JD said, and Dr. Ghoshal said there was no need to worry about that. "Thinking isn't doing, Jogen," he said. "We're not our thoughts." He said the important thing was to make sure we weren't missing any cues. And he thought we hadn't. He said we could all help her realize that a bad thought was just that—a bad thought. Just a thought, nothing more than that. Nothing that could do us any harm. So there was no need for her to be scared of an unpleasant thought even when it was about death. And no need for *us* to be scared of Zoya talking about death. "The mind is growing," he said. "It's exploring new terrains of experience. There will be questions, often difficult ones. We have to be careful we don't end up pathologizing normal behavior." He insisted we didn't need more than one more session with him.

Our final appointment with Dr. Ghoshal was in early March, a good three weeks after the second session. And it was during this time I'd seen the first signs of hope. The gap between Zoya's questions about pain, old age and death had started to increase. It was between three and six days now, which was a huge improvement. What happens to the body if someone dies? she asked one day. It rots, I told her. Dr. Ghoshal had said we needed to be honest in our answers. And I told her about the customs through which different communities deal with their dead. Which was the hard part. She couldn't believe birds would eat the body of her father, and JD's would be burned. Somehow, burial seemed more acceptable. But the weight of so much earth? That bothered her.

Under the white cotton sheet, our naked bodies touched one another along the flanks. The sweat that had covered them moments ago fast evaporating, our breathing back to its normal rhythm. We lay staring at the ceiling as the AC whirred softly. The light on the night table on JD's side of the bed was on.

"I'm almost scared to confess it," I said.

"What?" JD turned on his side and propped his head on his left hand.

"That I'm not scared anymore."

He smiled.

"For the first time since December. I can see the nightmare fading. I can see light at the end of the tunnel. Dr. Ghoshal was so right. Didn't he say...whatever the trigger was, it was going to lose its effect soon? It's been a month since we saw him last and look how things have changed. It doesn't happen more than once a week these days. It's almost unbelievable."

"You're right."

"So, maybe there's no need for us to see any other doctor? Maybe you should stop trying to get in touch with this young psychiatrist?"

"I forgot to tell you that I just heard from her. She'll be back in May and will let me know when she is. But if you think there's no need to see her—"

"Do *you* think there's any?"

"Well, I just thought...why not get a second opinion? You know? From a younger professional. Just to make sure everything is *really* okay. You know what I mean?" He stroked my hair. "It's not as if...I don't have enough faith in Ghoshal Uncle. As I've said many times before, I think he's very, very good." He paused. "I just wanted to make sure we've looked at *everything* there is to look at. You know? Make sure we aren't missing anything."

"Are we missing anything?"

"I hope not," he said.

The heat has been unbearable since the middle of March. It's the beginning of May and the temperature has already reached the upper 30s. The forecast for next week is worse; it will be 45 degrees or more in some parts of West Bengal. There will be reports of heat-related deaths from across the state, maybe many more this year than before. Over the last few days, all I've heard people talk about—at work, in shops, on the street—is the nor'wester, the *Kalboishakhi*. For all the damage it does, it also brings relief from the heat ahead of the monsoon. And right now, that's the one thing that seems to be on everyone's mind—relief from the heat.

Zoya is worried about Ramu and his mother and sister. The heat is one thing, but how will they cope with a storm? What will happen to the few things they have? The pots and the pans, the pieces of rags they've gathered together to soften the concrete on which they sleep, their pile of bags and the blue sheet of plastic, their roof—it'll be the first thing to go if a storm breaks out. Since they came and settled on that spot on the pavement in mid-February, there's been a couple of rain showers, but no storm. And Zoya doesn't want any. No matter how awful the heat is, she doesn't want the rains to come until Ramu and his family have found a home.

"It's a good thing Zoya worries about Ramu and his family," Dr. Ghoshal had said to us. "It shows she has an empathetic mind."

The boy must be fifteen or sixteen, and his sister four or five years younger, although she looks much smaller than a girl that age. She's as skinny as their mother, who looks years older than she is. I've had to ask the boy his name, and his sister's—Zoya wanted to know. And once she got to know their names, she started insisting we send them food every day. "No, not every day, Zoya," I'd say to her, annoyed by her doggedness. Although, since then, we've been doing it fairly regularly, dropping off small bags of leftovers, or packets of uncooked rice, lentils, and potatoes every few days. Along with a bit of money, usually about ten rupees; sometimes a bit more, sometimes less. And every day, several times a day, Zoya stands at the living-room window looking down at the blue plastic-covered corner of the pavement. Sometimes, on her way back from school, she'd linger a few moments at the entrance to our building to wave at them.

"Where is Ramu and Laxmi's father?" Zoya asks.

"I don't know, sweetheart."

"Why don't you ask them?"

"I cannot. It's inappropriate to ask such questions."

"What is *ini...propiate*?"

"Not polite."

"Are they poor because their father is not there?"

I'm trying to come up with an answer when JD walks in. Every time he walks into a room, he displaces a volume of space in the minds of the people there. A bit like that story of Archimedes getting into his bathtub. Except, in this case, the displaced space is far more than the volume of his body. At least that's how I feel. That's the kind of hopeless bathtub my mind is when it comes to this man.

"Didn't mean to interrupt," he says. "Just wanted to find out what you wanted for dinner. There's a cloud buildup, so we should hurry up."

Fifteenth day today. And JD can barely hide his excitement. He's perky like a little boy. He's been that way all day long.

"Don't we do Mocambo every time we're happy?" I smile.

"Mocambo it will be then." JD takes a mock bow, making Zoya giggle. "And the same dishes, of course?"

I nod and smile, throwing him a kiss. Zoya does the same.

After dinner, I get Zoya ready for bed. She doesn't like the AC, so we always leave at least one of her widows open during the summer months. Unless it rains. And today it hasn't, despite the cloud buildup. I tuck her into bed and kiss her goodnight. I turn out the lights in her room and, walking out, close the door behind me.

Walking to the living room, I feel the pull of an eagerness I haven't felt in a very long time. I cannot wait to join JD. I cannot wait for us to start celebrating what feels almost like the resumption of life itself.

He hands me my glass. "Fifteen days," he says.

"Fifteen days," I say, tears starting to roll down my face.

He puts down his glass and steps closer to hold me in his arms.

We stand like that for a while, not saying a word. Just being close, both to each other and to the moment. And feeling grateful. And *yes*, happy, too. Then I hear it—from within the folds of JD's arms and the wheeze of his alcohol-quickened breath. It takes me a moment to realize it's a human scream. And then I recognize Zoya's voice in it. My heart misses a beat. A chill runs down my spine. I drop my glass to the floor and tear myself out of JD's arms, and rush to her room.

Zoya's body is bunched up against the corner of her headboard, her shriek piercing every living cell in mine. I see something dark lying close to where her head was on the bed. It's a bat. Lying in a pool of blood on the pink linen sheet. Its wings twitching a few times and then falling perfectly still. The poor creature must have strayed into the room through the open window and flown into the ceiling fan.

I pick Zoya up and carry her out of the room as JD walks in. He steps aside to let us pass.

"Is the bat dead?" she asks.

I pretend not to hear her as I push open the door to my room.

"Mama, is the bat dead?"

"Yes, it is," I say, my body beginning to shake as violently as hers.

A MINUTE'S SILENCE

Himadri Sanyal planned his death and its immediate aftermath as carefully as he'd planned every important event of his adult life. Nothing was going to be left to chance, or to the whims of those who would be in charge of things after he was gone. All that would happen after his passing, if it involved him—his life, his death—it had to happen the way *he* wanted it to happen. And he wanted to do everything he could to make sure it did. *How you leave is a mark of how you lived*, he said to himself.

Returning from the doctor's office Tuesday afternoon, he asked Radha, his housekeeper and cook, to make him a cup of tea, the doctor's familiar voice still ringing in his ears with those unfamiliar words: "Lung cancer." "Stage 4." "I'm sorry!" Words he realized he hadn't yet absorbed the full meaning of, the *totality* of what they implied, although everything suddenly seemed different now. The way things looked, the spaces and objects around him, and the play of light, and the sounds coming in through the windows—voices, traffic, birds— all so familiar, yet somehow different. Different from how they were just hours ago, as he was getting ready to leave for Dr. Mukherjee's office. As if a curtain had fallen between him and his world, making it look and sound and feel like it wasn't quite his.

"Thank you," he said to Radha with a nod as she set the cup of tea on the table next to him. A breeze lifted the curtain on the window. Somewhere close by, two people were laughing loudly. Himadri cleared his throat. "I don't need the biscuits," he said to Radha. She asked if she could bring him anything else: "A piece of toast? Some muri-chanachur?" He shook his head, and before she closed the door behind her, said that he didn't want to be disturbed as long as he was in the study.

After she left the room, he bolted the door. Something he'd never done before—it had always been enough to tell Radha he didn't want to be interrupted. Then he switched off his cell phone and put the landline phone off the hook, and sat down in his reading chair. All his life, Himadri had been known for his fortitude. People praised him for that, which sometimes filled him with an energy, a sense of largeness inside his chest that was embarrassingly close to pride. *But where was it now?* Where could he look for fortitude when the thought of his imminent end made his inside feel like an antacid tablet in a glass of water? The core of his being rapidly dissolving, his sense of who he was untethered from his flesh. He'd never had a shortage of crises in life, but nothing had ever made him feel that way before.

The curtain billowed again and the breeze felt cooler. Himadri coughed. Outside, the men continued to laugh. He coughed again, a deeper one this time—it rose from his chest and lingered for a few moments. His body shook, the soreness in his chest spreading like ripples. He leaned forward in the chair, his elbows on the armrests, and breathed as slowly as he could. Memories of the past flashed in his mind like in a slide show. He'd read somewhere that the brains of those nearing death replay past experiences, pulling out lived moments from the archives of oblivion to show the soon-to-be-departed their life in a final flashback. He knew he wasn't yet close enough to that moment to have such an experience, but he was having it anyway. The faces of his mother and father—he'd lost them both a month and a half before the release of his first ever feature film. They'd died just three weeks apart—first she, then he.

And fittingly, his film had flopped. Most of the critics of Calcutta had ignored it completely, and those who wrote about it didn't have anything good to say. The review in *The Asian Age* was so damning it had made his wife, Bonolota, break down in tears while reading it. "Why should the critics' opinions hurt us if we don't agree with them?" he'd said to her, although he'd partly agreed with *one* of them. "A slightly faster pace wouldn't have been so bad after all," he'd confessed to his wife. "The story wouldn't have changed, and it might have seemed more appealing to some. And at least one good cinema hall might have shown it for a week or two."

Even though he mostly disagreed with the few who'd reviewed the film, and didn't take their remarks to heart, he'd read their judgements with care, parsing them for meaning that could shed light on aspects of his own work, and filmmaking in general, which he might not have been attentive to. He'd cut out the review articles, marking sentences and paragraphs, and put them away in his notebook. He'd taken notes like a student, underlining words and phrases—"dialog", "extreme long shots", "eye level", "low key lighting", "non-diegetic sound". He'd met failure with humility and ardor, vowing to do better in the future. And he *had* done better. The next film, during the making of which he'd faced some of his worst nightmares—the cameraman had a heart attack on the set, and the producer, whom Himadri had known to be a kind and reasonable man, immediately left the project, which at that point was only about halfway through—but in spite of that, and other production-related problems, and a protracted battle with the censor board and a hugely delayed release, the film had received reasonably good reviews. As had his next two films. But success, in terms of his pictures running in the cinemas and people watching them in large numbers and talking about them, had continued to elude him. Himadri had stayed undaunted. He knew that the path he'd chosen was a difficult one. The nature of the art form was such that he could never be in charge of everything. For his work to come into being and find acceptance and recognition, it had to depend on agency completely beyond his control. But to things that were within his control, he'd always given his absolute best, no matter how difficult the circumstances.

The sun had set. The study was almost entirely engulfed in darkness. In her room Radha blew her conch shell three times. Himadri kept sitting in his chair, the teacup on the table next to him untouched. In his mind, a stampede of long-forgotten moments from his school and college life. Class trips to the zoo, the botanical gardens, Puri, Darjeeling. The heady days of radical student politics—the slogans, the demonstrations, the *rage*. How he and his comrades wanted to change the world, and *believed* they could! The many losses in love and life, and the few triumphs—having Bonolota by his side as a partner, having a son like Ronojoy, and a small circle of loyal friends. All these thoughts and memories, with their cargo of feelings, images, sounds, and words, came flooding in. And the face of Bonolota—those eyes of hers and their endless depths. Himadri imagined her looking at him now, knowing what she would have known if she hadn't gone before him.

The death of his wife had been the biggest loss in Himadri's life. A loss from which he'd often thought he would never recover. He'd felt as if he was alive despite having been sliced in half with almost all his lifeblood drained out. He was so close to death emotionally that he'd lost all fear of it. So it wasn't the fear of death that gripped him now. It was sadness. A profound sense of melancholy brought on by the realization that the life he loved, for all its inherent suffering, its almost unbearable burden of dukkha, was soon going to be over. That the story of Himadri Sanyal was fast drawing to a close, his cherished private project of being human as completely as possible rudely aborted. He wished he had a bit more time; a few more years—*was that asking too much?* Even a year or two might have given him the time he needed to tie up the loose ends of his life, his career—to put the finishing touches to what might have been his legacy.

The new film that he'd been waiting to start shooting; he could finish it in a year's time. But that was not to be. According to Dr. Mukherjee, he had between six and eight months. This wasn't like any adversity Himadri had faced before. Against the harshest storms of life, his core had always held firm—unruffled, tranquil. And it was this doggedly equanimous self of his that had been the one inexhaustible source of strength that he could always count on. Now that the body that held it was about to be perished, his reservoir of fortitude evaporated, Himadri didn't know where to turn for the comfort he needed. He didn't believe in afterlife, like the

Charvakas of ancient India whom he championed. For him, as for those materialists of long ago, there was no god, no soul. And no illusion of continuation after death. He felt like a desert oasis with its last drops drying up, unable to quench its own thirst.

A koel sang in the darkness. Himadri remembered how his wife loved hearing the bird at night. *Bonolota,* he muttered, his eyes welling up. *Only darkness now....*

He wept as the evening thickened around him.

The cough kept him awake most of the night. Between bouts of coughing, each one of which seemed to last a little longer than the ones the night before, Himadri thought about how he'd failed to take in most of Dr. Mukherjee's explanations about his condition. In people with limited metastasis, the variability in stage 4 survival rates is reasonably wide, he remembered the doctor saying. "But, unfortunately, that's not the case with you." With those words, the young doctor had thrown a shroud of incomprehension over Himadri's mind. Nothing else he said penetrated that. Phrases like "distant lymph nodes", "liver and bones", "pain in the upper right arm and upper leg" were sounds devoid of meaning. They impinged on his eardrums like empty tin cans, bouncing off the walls of his mind without leaving any impression there. Then there were words, long strings of them, that he didn't even register. He'd already understood the gist of the outcome; the finer details were irrelevant.

In six months—eight, if he was lucky—he would be gone. But he had at least that much time to write the final act of his life, shape it exactly the way he wanted to. Which, it suddenly occurred to him, was so much better than not having that opportunity. It was as if he was in a car speeding toward the edge of a cliff and had seen the danger sign just in time to know what lay ahead. And being forewarned about the impending end seemed somewhat more benign than an unprepared drop into it. While his body readied itself for the exit, suffering the pain and indignity of a dying body, his mind could draw the strands of his story together, explaining whatever needed to be explained about the plot prior to its erasure. Before becoming part of the infinity, he could timestamp his here-and-now the way he wished.

It was a few minutes past four in the morning when he decided to get out of bed. The coughing had eased by then, but he wasn't sleepy anymore. Not wanting to wake Radha, Himadri went to the kitchen as quietly as he could and made himself a cup of tea. Then he sat at his desk to write an email to Ronojoy, who lived in America.

Dear Rono, he wrote on his laptop. *I hope you and Jill are well. I went to Dr. Mukherjee's office yesterday. He thinks that the problem has worsened, and he's changed the medication and asked me to see him once every ten days or so. No need to panic, however. I have pledged total compliance with the doctor. I shall do everything I'm asked to do. But if you can, try and take some time off and come here for a short visit. Three weeks should be enough. Please try to arrive by the end of October, and you must bring Jill along. I'm not writing to her separately, but please tell her it's important. With warmest regards, Baba.*

In an hour or so, Ronojoy called. He worked at an energy consulting firm in Boston and Jill, Jill Bradley, the woman he'd been living with for over two years, was a freelance web designer.

"What exactly did Dr. Mukherjee say?" Ronojoy asked, clearly worried.

"There was no need to call," Himadri replied. "I sent you the email so we could avoid a long-distance call."

"What did the doctor say?"

"What—" Himadri coughed. "You know how—" he coughed some more. As he cleared his throat after a pause and prepared to start talking again, he had another coughing fit.

Ronojoy waited as his father tried to stop coughing. "Please put down the phone, Baba," he said after a few moments. "I'll call you later." But instead of calling his father back, he called the doctor later in the morning and found out the real reason behind his father's email.

"I know," Ronojoy said the next time he was on the phone with his father, which was several hours later. "Dr. Mukherjee has told me everything."

"Oh, you talked to him?" Himadri said softly. He yawned; he'd gone off to sleep sitting at his desk. "Yes, my time is up," he continued after a pause. "After your mother's death, I lost all fear of death. And I also stopped thinking about it. In a strange way, death was like a bond, an insurance policy, that you knew would mature at some point in the future...but you didn't think about it. Then one day, you suddenly discover that the date of maturity is here."

"That's a strange analogy."

"I know, and that's because the maturity date has opposite meanings in these—" Himadri coughed; after a brief pause, he cleared his throat and continued, "maturity has opposite meanings in these two things—in one it's the accumulation of value...and it's depletion in the other. But your day-to-day life is blind to both processes." He paused again to clear his throat. "Anyway, there are things that need our urgent attention now. I can take care of most of them myself, but for some I need your help. Which is why I asked you to come as soon as possible. It would be wonderful if you could come in a week or two, but I know you cannot. So, October is fine—the second or the third week. It gives you roughly two and a half months. And I won't die in two and a half months, I can promise you that." He chuckled weakly.

"Let's try and talk tomorrow," Ronojoy said. "I don't want you to start coughing again. Get some rest now."

"I know it won't be easy for you to make this trip," Himadri continued, "but you should try as hard as you can."

"I will."

Switching off the phone, Himadri found Radha standing at the door with a flask and a glass in her hand. He'd forgotten to bolt the door and wondered if she'd overheard the conversation. Although they'd spoken mostly in English, both had used enough Bengali for Radha to understand what they were talking about. Besides, she knew the family well enough to grasp things based only on how they sounded. He felt intruded on and exposed, and suddenly angry because of that. He didn't want her to find out about his condition, at least not yet.

"The cough is getting worse," she said.

"You should've knocked." His voice didn't hide the annoyance he felt.

"It was a mistake," Radha said meekly, setting the flask and the glass down on his desk. "Both hands were occupied, so I cleared my throat. You didn't hear."

Morning light was pouring through the window that faced the backyard of the next house. Crows were cawing.

A sparrow chirped busily just outside the window. Himadri was surprised how quickly the room had turned bright.

"Bay leaf and ginger tea," Radha said pointing at the flask. "There's some clove and honey too. Good for the cough. I'll do it every morning." Then, turning to leave, she said, "You're coughing too much."

"There was no need to take so much trouble," Himadri said, now feeling guilty. "You should've stayed in bed a bit longer. You never get enough rest."

"Don't worry about me," she said, walking out of the room, "please drink the tea," closing the door behind her.

Himadri prepared two lists. One for himself, with things needed to be accomplished before his son arrived, and the other for his son, which listed tasks to be carried out after his death. But Durga Puja was in early October, which meant he had even less time to finish doing all he wanted to do before Ronojoy's arrival. Although Puja was roughly a week-long affair, it came with clouds of gaiety (which Himadri always interpreted as emotional versions of the cotton ball clouds one found in the autumn sky) that disrupted normal life on either side of the event. The pace of work at the courts, the Calcutta Municipal Corporation and other government offices, annoyingly sluggish in normal, non-festive times of the year, became almost nonexistent weeks before the Puja started. "Not now, come back after Puja" was a line Himadri had heard all his adult life. Also, "Wait, Puja is only just over—give us some time! Are we humans or what?"

Himadri wrote a one-and-a-half-page letter by hand to the director of the Indian Museum, saying he wanted to donate his entire collection of masks. He mentioned a

Tibetan death mask, a very old Gambhira dance mask, a Mahakala, and several pieces from Indonesia, Sumatra, Benin and Congo, pointing out how old and rare they were. Next in his to-do list were messages to be sent to the All India Radio for his collection of LP records of Hindustani music, the Asiatic Society for his books on colonial history, and the Satyajit Ray Film and Television Institute for his videocassettes and books on cinema.

Himadri finished writing all the letters over the next two days, and faxed them one by one. He wrote that he was donating his collections to ensure their proper storage and care, which he said he couldn't do because of a lack of space and his old age. Radha said she didn't understand why he was working so hard when he was more unwell than he'd ever been. "There will be enough time for work," she said. "Take rest now." She made him a fresh flask of tea three times a day, and walked into the study every time he had a coughing attack.

The heads of those institutions, except only the Asiatic Society, responded within two weeks. They were both interested and grateful. A week or so later, the first group of people arrived to pack things into crates and boxes. It was a Monday, the 25th of August. By the middle of September, the house had started to look like a place soon to be abandoned.

Himadri could hear Radha sobbing in the kitchen. "What is happening here?" she said when she saw him. "Does Chotobabu know?" She called Rono Chotobabu. "Only the books and the masks," Himadri said, hoping that would comfort her. "Nothing will happen to your part of the house."

He'd already put some money in Radha's bank account to make sure she wouldn't have to look for work after his death. She'd come to the house as an aya shortly after Ronojoy's birth thirty-six years ago, and stayed on to become an inseparable part of the family. She'd lost her husband early and had no family of her own. After Bonolota's death, it was she who'd steadied the domestic boat, taking full charge of the household. In his will Himadri had divided the house between his son and Radha, giving her part of the first floor. He'd registered the will years ago and put it in the custody of his lawyer.

He put two photocopies of the document in a folder meant for his son. He wrote letters, sealed them in envelopes with names and addresses and appropriate postage on the ones to be mailed posthumously, and left instructions for the ones to be hand-delivered. He sat at his desk for some time every day, writing mostly by hand and sometimes on the laptop, and striking off items on his list one by one. *No response yet from the Asiatic Society!* he kept thinking in the midst of all that activity, although he knew it was hardly unusual for such organizations to not respond promptly, and that they might get back to him at some point in the future and agree to accept his offer. But *the future* had very little meaning to Himadri now. Anything happening later than a few days or weeks, no matter how desirable the outcome, was decidedly beyond the time frame of relevance. He wasn't an impatient man by nature; he just didn't have what it took to be patient. *Time.*

He thought about asking Buddhadeb, a retired professor of history and one of his four closest friends, if he knew anyone at the Asiatic Society who could help. But he decided against it because he'd have to tell his friend the truth to explain the urgency, and he didn't want to do that. Like the other three, Buddhadeb was a few years older than Himadri, and in frail health. There was no point in burdening him with the news just yet. Instead, on his list, next to the item reading *All books on colonial history to Asiatic Society*, Himadri wrote, *Moved to Rono's list* and added the task to the list meant for his son with the note *Brown almirah (83 titles). Reference: Himadri Sanyal's letter (to AS) of August 4, 2008.*

It was the beginning of September. Since the diagnosis in late July, contrary to the promises he'd made to himself and his son, Himadri had been to the doctor's office only twice, and that too with much reluctance. He refused radiation therapy and didn't see any point in seeing the doctor as frequently as he'd been advised. Now that he'd come to terms with the fact of his death, it made no sense to waste whatever time he had left undergoing therapy that would only prolong his suffering. He would rather spend the time attending to the tasks he needed to finish. And despite his frequent coughing fits, constant headache and increasing weakness, plus the monsoon and the Puja-related disruptions, Himadri had managed to accomplish almost all his tasks. He'd taken care of his tax returns, terminated a life insurance policy, and withdrawn a fixed deposit that didn't have Ronojoy's name as a nominee and transferred the money to an account that did.

There was no need to meet anyone anymore. And he avoided talking on the phone as much as he could. He kept his cell phone mostly switched off, and rarely picked up the other phone. All he needed to do now was wait—wait for his son. He had just enough strength left for that.

Saturday evening, he switched on the cell phone to see if his son had tried to call. It was almost five thirty, and about eight in the morning in Boston. Ronojoy usually called around that time. The phone rang almost as soon as Himadri turned it on. It was Anirban, his director of photography. They'd been working together for years. "Yes, Anirban," Himadri said, hoisting himself slowly to sit on the edge of the bed; he'd been lying there all day. He shifted the body weight from one side of his seat to the other and back, looking for a posture that would hurt less. "How are you?" Anirban asked. He knew Himadri hadn't been keeping well. He said he'd tried to reach him several times over the past few days, and asked if he could see him. Anirban's excitement about the project had been soaring since the purchase of the film rights to the story. Basant Shroff wanted to make it a big-budget film, which would be a first for Himadri. And a first for Anirban, too. Basant was Himadri's producer; he believed it was only a matter of time before one of his films became a box-office hit. "Maybe this one, who knows!" he said. He was so optimistic he'd approached the great Raj Kulkarni for the lead role. A Bollywood star with a background in Marathi theater and arthouse cinema. The actor had reviewed the screenplay and agreed to play the role. And they were expecting him to confirm within the next two or three months.

"Better this way than me dropping dead in the middle of a shoot, isn't it?" Himadri said to Anirban when he came to the house next morning. "Like Guru Bakshi, the first cameraperson of my second picture. You know the story. And unlike then, the producer isn't leaving either. I've talked to Basant and Raj. Both are staying. Just some extra paperwork—Basant will take care of that. You have nothing to worry about." Himadri paused. "And as for me... I know I'm handing over the reins to someone who's better... *much* better... than I could ever be."

***

Ronojoy and Jill arrived in Calcutta on a Sunday. It was the 9th of November. By then, most of Himadri's valuables had found their foster homes. Of the things that remained were a few oil and watercolor paintings, a couple of framed photographs, a very old Naga death mask, which had been Ronojoy's favorite since his school days, and an almirah of books. And a Hasselblad 500EL Himadri had bought in Berlin many years ago, and a dozen or so undeveloped rolls of film he'd exposed using that camera. He placed the rolls in a plastic bag with a note for Ronojoy saying, *Maybe trash, maybe not—up to you to decide if you want to find out.* He and Jill would also have to decide what to do with all the photo albums, clothes, jewelry, and other family heirlooms. They could take with them whatever they wanted, and leave the rest here and enjoy them whenever they came to Calcutta.

Himadri wrote all that down on his letterhead and placed the pages in a large folder with the words *For Rono* on the cover.

***

"Why's everything gone from the house?" Ronojoy said the morning after his arrival.

He was shocked. As if the looming tragedy of his father's death would have been more bearable if the house didn't look so empty. As if the familiarity of the place, and the familiar ways in which it had always been filled with things he knew all his life, was what he was hoping to be comforted by. The lack of that seemed almost as cruel as the loss he was about to suffer.

Himadri tried to explain why he'd decided to give those things away. "Who would look after them?" he said. "They'd just sit here and rot. If you came back to India in a few years, I wouldn't have done this. But I know you won't. And why should you? You worked hard to have the life you have. There's no reason for you to give it up." Himadri paused, breathing with effort. He inhaled slowly through his nose and opened the mouth to exhale. After a few moments, he smiled and said, "Unless you decide to start a new life as a winemaker in the south…as some NRIs have done. But even then, you won't live here."

Ronojoy kept quiet. Sitting in the chair facing his father's desk, he looked around the room. The empty shelves, the discolored patches on the walls where many of the masks had hung, the few remaining paintings and photographs, an empty almirah with a single mask (it was that tribal mask from Nagaland he loved), a bookcase, and the skin-and-bones shadow of the man sitting across the table from him, and the hazy November light that lit up the room. A house lizard raced across the wall in front of him. It caught an insect where the wall met the ceiling and hid behind a faded black & white picture of Kanchanjangha. A brief rustling sound of the insect's wings and a thud or two of the lizard's body against the back of the photograph, then all was quiet again. It was like something straight out of one of his father's films. So unbearably gloomy that Ronojoy wanted to get up and walk out of the room, as he'd done more than once while watching his father's work.

"You won't have any reason to come and live here after I'm gone," Himadri said. "I know it, you know it. That's why giving those things away was the right thing to do."

"Look," Ronojoy said after a few moments, "it's fine with me. That you gave all this stuff away."

"You *knew* that I was going to do that, didn't you?"

"I did." Ronojoy nodded. "It's just that...I don't know...I guess I wasn't quite prepared to find you, and the house, in this state." He paused and looked away. Then, looking at his father, he said, "And I never saw your point in refusing the radiation therapy."

"Rono," Himadri smiled weakly, "it's too late to talk about that. Let's not waste time discussing what we should have or could have done. There's a lot that needs to be done *now*."

Ronojoy had never known his father to be a dominating character, intellectually or otherwise. And he was not, either at home or outside. Quite the opposite, in fact, he'd always been flexible, lenient and conciliatory both with those close to him and those who weren't. And yet, astonishingly, he always managed to have the last word in most things.

Next morning, after breakfast, Jill went back to the bedroom with a headache. She'd been struggling to get over jet lag. After helping Radha clear the dining table, Ronojoy came and sat down in his chair. Himadri was still seated in his.

"You need a shave," Ronojoy said, pouring tea in his father's cup from the pot Radha had just brought to the table.

"Do I?" Himadri wheezed, rubbing his chin. "Normally, I shave every other day."

Ronojoy nodded. Both drank their tea quietly. Somewhere in the neighborhood a Hindi film song was playing on loudspeakers. Ronojoy vaguely remembered the song. Outside the window, which overlooked the backyard of a newly built four-story apartment building, a single crow cawed nonstop. It was sitting on a mango tree, the only tree to survive the construction of the new building. Ronojoy remembered the time when that backyard was full of trees—two or three krishnachuras, a gigantic neem tree, a few guavas and that mango, among many others that he didn't know the names of—which he and his neighborhood friends climbed all the time. The only friend of his who didn't like climbing trees was Gautam, whose family owned the property—the entire compound with all those trees and a big house in the middle where they lived.

One Saturday morning, when they went to Gautam's house, they found the front door locked. Ronojoy and three of his friends were sitting on one of the lower branches of the krishnachura close to the front verandah of Gautam's house, when his parents returned and asked the boys to go home. Gautam wasn't well, they'd been told. Three days later, he died. And that was the end of Ronojoy's boyhood. He rarely met his other friends after that, and never went back to that garden again. Although it was right there behind his house, that sanctuary of past joy and tranquility—a constant reminder of what he'd lost. Over the years, every time he stood at the living room window, or the one in his father's study, looking out at the steadily thinning patch of greenery, he thought about his friend, and how his death had permanently closed a chapter of his life. There was a picture of Gautam in one of their photo albums, one of those red-hued color photographs from the early 80s. He'd come to Ronojoy's house after school to show his newly updated album of cricket players' photos—he'd got a new picture of W.G. Grace, and one each of Clyde Walcott and Frank Worrell.

The two of them had this hobby of collecting pictures cut out of sports magazines. In the photograph, Gautam had his album held to his chest. Ronojoy's father had taken the picture with a big camera he'd brought from a recent trip to Europe.

Himadri cleared his throat. "I had a lingering fear that it might be cancer," he said, sounding like he was trying to hide his breathlessness. "But didn't think it would be at such an advanced stage. And that I'd have so little time left. I thought I might be able to finish shooting the new film. We were just waiting for Raj to confirm his dates." After a pause he smiled and said, "But life's like that. It sends you packing when it's done with you. Whether or not *you* are done with it."

Ronojoy wanted to bring up the subject of therapy again. *You could easily have a few more months*, he wanted to tell his father, but didn't. "More tea?" he asked.

Himadri shook his head. "I'll go lie in bed for some time," he said. "Sitting in a chair for too long isn't all that easy."

"Do you need help?" Ronojoy asked as Himadri pushed the chair back to stand up.

"This much I can still do myself. You go take a look at Jill and see if she's alright."

As his father shuffled his way out of the room, Ronojoy felt a stab of guilt for not having tried harder to make this trip earlier. Things would certainly have been more difficult at work if he'd left last month, there would have been more pressure on his team. But he might have found the old man in a slightly better shape, and they could have had a bit more time together.

Later in the day, Ronojoy called Dr. Mukherjee to ask him if he could suggest something to help ease his father's condition. Just to make it slightly less painful for him, he said. "Nothing but the most basic forms of palliative care, I'm afraid," the doctor answered. "Pain killers, which he's already been taking for some time. I can increase the dose. And home oxygen therapy. I'd definitely recommend that." Dr. Mukherjee sounded more remote than before, his tone noncommittal, as if he'd given up on his patient and no longer cared how he was. Ronojoy could tell that his father's refusal to comply with the doctor's advice had played its role. It had changed the relationship between them, which, just like his decline, seemed irreversible.

Jill took a few days to recover from jet lag. It was only on Friday that week that she'd woken up feeling rested. Ronojoy had finished a few chores in the meantime, the first of which was setting up oxygen therapy at home. He also bought a walker for his father, which Himadri said reminded him of his childhood. "The first steps into life are a lot like the last ones out of it," he said. "Both need support." It took him some time to get used to the walker, and the nasal cannula attached to a fifty-foot-long hose. But now he could walk from one room to another with a bit more comfort, and didn't run out of breath in the middle of every sentence. Although that hardly hid the fact that his condition was rapidly worsening.

"It can happen any day," Ronojoy said to Jill one night. They'd just come into their bedroom after dinner, which they'd had on their own and mostly in silence. Himadri had already gone to bed.

"He's changed so much," Jill said. "In the three and a half weeks that we've been here."

Ronojoy nodded.

"He hardly talks now."

"He talks, but less than before."

"Much less," Jill said.

"Much less." Ronojoy nodded. "The first few days he talked nonstop. You could hardly get a word in edgeways."

"He had things to tell you."

"He did. Things about, you know...things that needed to be done. All the lists, folders and documents. Details about the bank account. The handwritten instructions for me, the letters, and the stuff in the house. The house itself. The will. Radha, the books, the Asiatic Society, his letter to them. People to be contacted. You know, all those things. He talked about his funeral too, the way it should be done. 'If I go while you're still here,' he said, 'don't do the Hindu thing at the crematorium.' 'No priests and pujas, please,' he said. 'Just a minute's silence before they put me in the incinerator.' He wanted to make sure there were no loose ends. That everything was the way he wanted it to be. Like he was directing a film and I was his assistant." Ronojoy paused. "He also asked about us."

"What did he ask?"

"He asked me if I was happy."

Jill sat down next to Ronojoy on the edge of the bed. She took his hand in hers.

"If I got what I'd wanted. He'd never asked such questions before. And he wanted to know if we had any plans, if we're going to get married. Start a family. 'Don't wait too long,' he said to me."

Jill motioned for him to stop, turning her head to the door. She'd heard Himadri coughing.

As they waited, the fan's whir filled the silence. When the coughing started again, Ronojoy rushed out of the room followed by Jill.

They found him sitting upright in bed, groggy from the effects of the sleeping pill he'd been given earlier in the evening. He coughed a few more times. Ronojoy bent down to take a close look at the cannula, making sure it was in place. He also checked the oxygen flow rate and the humidifier bottle, and stood next to the bed. Jill stood next to him, holding his hand. After a few moments, he put his arms around his father, as if he were a child, and laid him gently down on bed, carefully adjusting the pillow to place Himadri's head exactly in the middle. He remembered his father doing the same things when his mother was on her deathbed. Day in and day out. Until she died.

Ronojoy had been doing this every night since the start of the oxygen therapy. Even if he didn't hear anything, he'd wake up in the middle of the night—at least once; some nights twice—and check on the old man. Getting ready for his trip a month or so ago, he hadn't thought he'd have so little time with his father, and so much of that would be spent in this manner. Himadri hadn't hidden the fact that he had stage 4 cancer. Besides, Ronojoy had also talked to the doctor. But none of that knowledge had quite prepared him for the situation in which they were now—not just him and his father, but also Jill. They'd planned to spend a month here, taking care of only the most urgent things, and return a fortnight before Christmas so that they could spend the holidays with her parents in Amherst. Then, depending on his father's condition, Ronojoy could come back in January for a brief visit on his own. But here they were, their original plans gone out of the window. Jill postponed her return till after Christmas, and Ronojoy kept his options open. He secretly dreaded being here by himself. Although he felt guilty for having dragged her into this grim episode of his life, he couldn't imagine what he'd do if she weren't by his side. And it was not just her physical presence that gave him strength, it was also how deeply she'd involved herself in the whole circumstance. By being what she'd been the past few weeks, Jill had dropped one more anchor into the depths of their intimacy, and it secured them more solidly to the ground of who they were as a couple.

"Do you want to marry me?" she asked one morning.

They were still in bed. Ronojoy was lying on his back, his eyes closed. He was awake but tired from insufficient sleep. He'd had to wake up twice that night. "What?" he said, opening his eyes and squinting at her. "What do you mean?"

"I mean, do you want to marry me?"

"Jill, sweetheart." He groaned. "Why now?"

"Do you or not?"

"I do, of course." He turned on his side to face her. "You *know* that!"

"Then let's get engaged."

"Yes, of course," he said. "We will."

"This weekend."

"Jill!" Ronojoy said. "What are you talking about?"

"We're getting engaged, Ron," she said calmly, placing her hand on his cheek. "We're not prepared, but we're going to do it. We're going to wing it. We're going to do it for him. For us. We're going to do it for the family."

He'd been planning to buy a ring and formally propose to her soon, and then throw a small engagement party. He'd targeted the beginning of the new year, sometime mid-January, right after Jill's birthday. He'd wanted it to be a surprise for her. But she beat him to it. When Himadri showed her all the jewelry he wanted her to have, she'd made up her mind. She wanted Ronojoy to put his mother's ring on her finger. And she'd picked out a simple gold ring that she was going to put on his.

They broke it to Himadri at the breakfast table. Even though he hardly ate any breakfast anymore, he tried to sit with them at the table as long as he could.

"Baba," Ronojoy said, his hand on his father's shoulder. "Jill and I have decided to get engaged."

"That's wonderful!" Himadri smiled, his eyes lit up.

"We'll do it here. On Saturday."

"This Saturday?" Himadri's voice shook with surprise. "Today is…?"

"Tuesday," Ronojoy said. "Three days is enough."

"Are you sure?" Himadri said. He looked at Jill.

"We are." Jill nodded. She reached across the table to hold his hand.

Tears began to trickle down Himadri's face. "Congratulations," he said, holding the hands of Jill and Ronojoy, and nodding his head. "You've made me…a very happy man." He smiled through his tears. "Old and sick, and dying, but very, very happy!"

Of Himadri's four closest friends, only Buddhadeb and Anil managed to attend the event on Saturday. Buddhadeb came with his wife Madhuri, and Anil came alone. The other guests were two of Ronojoy's school friends and their wives, a cousin and an old uncle, who'd been close to the family, and Anirban. Ten people, excluding Radha and the three of them. Madhuri helped Jill wear a sari, the red wedding Benarasi of Ronojoy's mother. "Thirty-seven years ago, I saw Bonolota in this sari," Madhuri said to Jill. "It looks just as pretty on you!" "You look wonderful tonight," Ronojoy whispered into Jill's ears. They exchanged rings and gave each other a kiss—quickly, awkwardly. Everyone clapped and raised a toast to them. "Thank you, Jill and Rono," Himadri said, his voice shaky but unusually high-pitched. "For deciding to get engaged here. I'm grateful! And I wish you two the very best in life. Be happy!" With a slightly trembling hand, he raised his glass to them, bowing his head to Jill and his son, tears rolling down his cheeks, and then tilted his head back to drop the rest of the drink into his mouth. With a paper napkin, Ronojoy gently wiped the dribble from his mouth and chin, and the tears from his face. "Javat jibet, sukham jibet," Himadri said, smiling, out of breath because he'd refused to wear his nasal cannula during the event. "As long as you live, live happily," he translated the Sanskrit phrase for Jill. "The Charvakas said that."

And for about two hours that evening, there was happiness in the house.

Himadri died the next day.

A little after six in the morning Radha woke Ronojoy to tell him that his father was unresponsive.

Ronojoy and Jill rushed to Himadri's room. "Baba?" he called, his head close to his father's. "Baba!" With the back of his hand, he stroked his father's stubbly cheek. It wasn't quite cold yet, but it was obvious he was gone. According to Dr. Mukherjee, who arrived half an hour later, Himadri might have died shortly before Radha went to his room. "Around five," he guessed. "Or maybe a bit earlier."

Either way, it didn't matter. Knowing the exact hour of his death made no difference to the fact of it. Ronojoy stood staring at his father's body. His head throbbed. The silence of the moment seemed as unreal as the sounds of last night, which still rang in his ears. Especially his father's voice—*Javat jibet, sukham jibet!*

"We have to hurry up," Jill whispered. She reminded him of Himadri's instructions about the funeral.

"Yes," Ronojoy nodded.

In his father's handwritten instructions, Ronojoy found the names and phone numbers of people who had to be contacted. Anirban was one of them. Ronojoy called him first. "Please keep it to yourself for now," he said to the shocked young man. "We have to try and make sure the press doesn't find out *before* the funeral. Baba left strict instructions. He didn't want any government body or people from Tollygunj to find out. He didn't want his death to be turned into a show. No need for anyone to pay their respects. Only the ones who were close to him."

There were phone numbers of two hearse rental services. Ronojoy called one of them. He read over the instructions several times to make sure he hadn't missed anything so all could be exactly as his father had wished. As if the old man was still in charge, keeping a close eye from his director's chair. Following his instructions accurately was Ronojoy's role, in which he wouldn't settle for anything less than a flawless performance. That was only how he could fully internalize his father's passing, and mourn it the way he could.

They reached the crematorium an hour and a half later. There was a long line of bodies waiting to be cremated. Thirteen of them, according to Anirban. "We're number fourteen," he said. "Shall we take the body out of the hearse?"

A man walked up to Ronojoy and introduced himself as Indra Thakur. "Secretary to the director of Nandan West Bengal Film Center," he said. "I got the news from Dr. Mukherjee, who's a good friend. And I came here half an hour ago. My condolences to you. It's a huge loss for all of us."

"Thank you." Ronojoy nodded. "But please try and keep your voice down. I don't want people to hear us."

The man nodded, throwing a quick glance around him. "I called Dr. Bhowmik, the director, and he was shocked to hear this," he continued in a hushed tone. "I'm sure he tried to reach you, too. In fact, he told me that he wished people had a chance to pay their last respects to Himadri-babu. And now that we have to wait our turn, we can actually do it. Please don't bring out the body yet."

"What do you mean?" Ronojoy frowned.

"I mean, since he cannot be cremated right now, why don't we allow people to pay their homage?"

"I'm afraid not," Ronojoy said. "My father was against this."

"I'm sure he was, because he was a humble man. But the fact remains that he was a leading light in the world of Bengali cinema. He was an integral part of the local industry. And the film fraternity here has the right to mourn his death just as much as his family does. I mean, he was one of us too, wasn't he?"

"You don't understand," Ronojoy said, a touch of annoyance in his voice. "My father left strict instructions against public mourning. There won't be any condolence meetings or anything. It was *his* own wish. And as his son, I don't want this to happen to him either."

"He was your father, of course," Indra Thakur persisted, "but he was also close to us. I have known Himadri-babu personally for more than fifteen years."

A crowd had gathered around them. It was mostly people waiting to cremate their dead. They stared at Jill. The fact that she, clearly a non-Indian, was at the crematorium piqued their curiosity. Ronojoy could hear people saying: "Who is it?" "Where's the body?" "Must be someone big!" "Must be related to this foreign lady!" "That man must be the son!"

Jill excused herself and took Ronojoy aside. "Don't get so worked up," she whispered. "I know Himadri hated the idea, but look at this."

"Each body will take about forty minutes," Anirban said. "So...more than eight hours. Even if they have both furnaces going, we'll be here for at least five hours."

"Right," Jill said.

"So?" Ronojoy said.

"So, we might as well do what this guy is saying."

"Are you out of your mind?"

"Think about it, Ron. Do you want to stand here for five hours? With all these bodies around you? And the crowd? And people screaming their heads off?"

"Plus, it's only a matter of time before the word gets out," Anirban said. "Someone will find out and then we'll have a mob to deal with."

A thick blanket of smoke came down from the incinerator chimneys, covering the entire area outside the cremation hall. Smoke billowed also from inside the hall, where bodies lay side by side on the floor, waiting to be put into the furnace. Stale wreaths were heaped high in one corner of the platform that led to the furnace area. The walls were covered with soot. Priests sat on the squalid floor conducting pujas that the relatives of the dead performed.

The smoke and its smell were suffocating. Men and women sat on the ground howling, their hands resting on the bodies of their loved ones. Others sat around with vacant looks on their faces. And there were those who looked completely unaffected by the reason that had brought them there. They milled around, talked loudly to one another and laughed. Some sat at the tea stalls across the narrow lane, drinking tea from earthen cups, smoking and chatting.

Two more bodies arrived, with them more people, who added to the commotion. Another swooping cloud of smoke drove Ronojoy and Jill further away from the cremation hall.

"This is really awful," Ronojoy said. "We can't do this for five hours."

"We'll both be sick."

"Unless we take him to another crematorium."

"Is there any?" Jill asked.

"Of course."

"But what's the guarantee things will be different there?"

"Right."

"I mean, we can't possibly spend the rest of the day running from one crematorium to another. Going to some stupid condolence meeting, or whatever it is they want us to go to, seems like a lesser evil. I don't know. But I'd much rather listen to platitude and empty eulogy than fill my lungs with the smoke of burning bodies."

"Alright, let's go."

"You're not angry, are you?" Jill asked, holding his hand.

Ronojoy wasn't angry. He just didn't like how things had turned out, as if his father's death the morning after their engagement wasn't bad enough. Now he couldn't even do the one thing he'd promised himself to do—making sure the funeral rites were conducted the way his father had wished.

Another noisy procession made its way into the compound. Young men with thin red cotton towels tied around their waist, screaming: *Bolo Hari, Hari Bol!*

Indra Thakur was talking on the phone. As he saw Ronojoy walking toward him, he disconnected the line. He knew he'd won the psychological tug of war. "I hope you have changed your mind, Mr. Sanyal?" he said even before Ronojoy had reached him. "I *knew* you would see our point and not deprive us of the opportunity to bid a proper farewell to Himadri-babu." There was triumph in his smile.

"Please make sure it's not too elaborate. We should try to come back in an hour or two."

"Yes, yes," the man said. "We'll wait for you in front of Nandan."

A crowd had gathered outside the film center. There were people waiting with wreaths and flowers in their hands. The body of Himadri Sanyal was taken down from the hearse and laid on the open porch. One by one, people stepped forward to place wreaths on his body. Next to it, a pile of flowers grew rapidly in size. The crowd swelled as people from film societies, cine clubs, and cultural organizations poured in to pay their homage. There were TV and newspaper reporters, along with politicians and people from the Tollygunj film industry, many of whom Ronojoy knew well. Basant Shroff was one of them. "What a tragedy!" he said, stepping close to Ronojoy. "I'd been really looking forward to him doing this new film. It would have finally given him what he always wanted and deserved." The director of Satyajit Ray Film and Television Institute gripped Ronojoy's hand and said, "A very sad day! We couldn't even thank him properly for his donation to the Institute." Dr. Bhowmik described his death as "an enormous loss, which will create a vacuum in the world of cinema in India". The state minister of information and culture called him "the pride of Bengal." Several actors talked about their experience of working with Himadri Sanyal. "He was not only a great director," one of them said, "but also a great human being."

Ronojoy stood in a corner with Jill, trying to avoid eye contact with people. Although he couldn't wait for the ceremony to end, and was ridden with guilt for having allowed it to happen, a part of him couldn't help feeling proud—proud of his father, whose shrunken face, with lumps of cotton in the nostrils, had almost entirely disappeared under the heap of flowers and wreaths. *As much as it's a show,* he thought to himself, and *it is a show—this public mourning of Himadri Sanyal's death—isn't it also a measure, maybe in a perversely roundabout way, and only to a small extent, of the value people attach to his work?* He thought about his father's lifelong regret—that his films never drew big crowds. That, and the irony of what was on display.

By the time they were back at the crematorium, the sun had started to set. Himadri's body was third in line.

The crowd had thinned to two or three small groups of people scattered across the compound. Of those who had come with Ronojoy and Jill in the morning, most had gone home. Anirban and two of his friends were the only ones left; they sat on the curb of an island of manicured garden surrounded by a fence.

Inside the cremation hall, Ronojoy and Jill stood in silence as Himadri's body waited its turn.

EUGENE DATTA

The author of the poetry collection *Water & Wave* (Redhawk, 2024), Eugene Datta has worked as a newspaper journalist, a book reviewer, and an editor. His fiction and poetry have appeared in publications such as *Common Ground Review*, *The Dalhousie Review*, *Mantis*, *Hamilton Stone Review*, *The Bangalore Review*, and elsewhere. A recipient of the Stiftung Laurenz-Haus fellowship, he has held residencies at Ledig House International Writers' Colony, and Fundación Valparaíso. Born and raised in India, he lives in Aachen, Germany. *The Color of Noon* is his debut collection of stories.

www.ingramcontent.com/pod-product-compliance
Lightning Source LLC
Chambersburg PA
CBHW021711190726
48289CB00008B/2472